P9-DCA-956

Other novels by the Author:

Troy

Perseus

Luna

Janey

Leslie

MEDEA

Richard Matturro

Drawings by
Mary Trevor Thomas

Livingston Press
The University of West Alabama

Copyright © 2014 Richard Matturro
All rights reserved, including electronic text
isbn 13: 978-1-60489-136-2, hardcover
isbn 13: 978-1-60489-137-9, trade paper
isbn: 1-60489-136-X, hardcover
isbn: 1-60489-137-8 trade paper
Library of Congress Control Number 2014932120
Printed on acid-free paper.
Printed in the United States of America by
EBSCO Media
Hardcover binding by: Heckman Bindery
Typesetting and page layout: Amanda Joy Nolin
Proofreading: Brianna Blue,
Breanna Black, Kimberlee Harrell, Tricia Taylor
Cover art, design, and layout: Mary Trevor Thomas

first edition
6 5 4 3 2 1

MEDEA

For Barbara Barclay

Contents

ὡς τρὶς ἂν παρ᾽ ἀσπίδα
στῆναι θέλοιμ᾽ ἂν μᾶλλον ἢ τεκεῖν ἅπαξ.

Euripides *Medea 250-251*

I
Witch

SHE WAS CROSS-EYED. The two lines of her vision bent inward upon each other and converged prematurely so that whenever she looked at you, her gaze appeared to be directed at something else, some invisible thing hovering in the vacant air between you. The defect suggested a half-wit, but behind the foreshortened stare lurked an inscrutable intelligence.

Her brother, Apsyrtus, spotted her at the far end of the garden, kneeling and tending her plants. Unobserved, he slipped down the path and casually leaned against the colonnade behind her. She was jabbing a trowel into the earth, aerating the soil around an evil-looking vine, its hairy tendrils clinging to the rough stones as it snaked its way up the wall. The chiton she wore hung loosely over a lean, muscular frame, her thin face hidden by a mane of black curls that brushed the ground as she worked. Lifting one of the pendulous blossoms, she examined the hidden stamen, shook a few, fine grains of yellow powder on the back of her hand. A bronze dagger flashed from her belt. With its razor edge she made a small longitudinal cut in the stem, then gently squeezed it with her fingertips until a pearl of milky liquid gathered in the slit. She collected the droplet into a vial.

"What's that stuff for?" Apsyrtus asked.

She glanced over her shoulder at him, her flawed brown eyes registering annoyance at the intrusion. "Choking."

"It prevents choking?"

"No, it *makes* you choke."

He snorted. "You're a witch, Medea."

"And you're ... up early."

"Father called a council meeting this morning. I don't know why he insists I go. He always tells me ahead of time I'm not to say anything."

"He probably has the naïve expectation that you'll learn something."

Apsyrtus yawned, watched idly as his sister slid over to the next vine, repeated the deft incision and forced out another bead of liquid. Offhandedly he said, "Father brought it up again."

"Did he?" Medea's tone affected a total lack of interest.

"Yesterday. He reminded me that I'm twenty-five. Then he ticked off the names of four girls from prominent families he'd consider 'acceptable.' Acceptable to him, that is. One of them is only thirteen, for God's sake!"

"Lucky you."

Abruptly he pushed away from the colonnade and straddled the path, blocking her way. "Father never pressures you to get married, and you're older than I am."

"That's because I'm crazy. Remember?"

"Yes, like a fox. You probably *could* get married if you really wanted to—if you were willing to make a little effort to act like everybody else. Men are afraid of you, growing this lethal shrubbery back here, and always carrying a knife."

Medea sat back on her heels and brushed a strand of hair from her forehead. "Men wear their desires like a leash. If I want a dog, I'll get a dog."

"Well, I don't have the luxury of a choice. As heir to the throne,

I have to get married. For me, getting some silly girl pregnant is a state duty. Father's worst fear is that I'll die before I have a son."

"You won't die unless I kill you." She rapped his shin with the blunt edge of her dagger. "Now get out of my way."

Apsyrtus stepped aside. "He panics at the thought of one of our nephews becoming king. The last thing he wants is someone with Greek blood sitting on the throne of Colchis."

"We all have Greek blood if you go back far enough. We speak Greek, don't we?"

"Yes, but not like Phrixus spoke Greek. He was *from* Greece."

Medea fell silent, her crooked gaze focused inward.

"Remember when he first came? I was just a kid, and I didn't care about the fleece at all. It was his accent that impressed me. Then you told me that we were the ones who spoke with an accent, not him, and I didn't believe you." Apsyrtus snorted. "Of course Father was quite willing to overlook his Greek blood in order to get the fleece."

"A lot of good it's done him."

"Your problem, Medea, is that you spend too much time buried in these ferns to know how the world works. The Golden Fleece has become the symbol of Colchis. Because of it, we're renowned everywhere."

"A jewel stuck on a toad's back would make the toad renowned too, and yet he'd still be a toad."

Apsyrtus eyed her for a moment. "He fancied you, didn't he?"

"I'm busy," she muttered, turning her attention back to the vine.

"I used to see how Phrixus looked at you, even though you were young and he was married to our sister. I know he fancied you."

"You don't know anything."

"Is that so? Well, I know something you don't. I found out why he came to Colchis."

The dagger stood motionless, its tip poised on the flesh of the stem. "Why?"

Apsyrtus let his knees buckle and dropped to a sitting position on the stone path next to her. "I talked to a trader recently from Beotia, his homeland. He told me that Phrixus was crown prince just like me, but after his mother died, his father remarried, and it seems the second wife accused Phrixus of something. I don't know if it was true or not, but the king believed it and sentenced him to die. So Phrixus ran off, and he ended up here, which is about as far away from Greece as you can go."

"What had he done?"

"The trader didn't know, but it must have been really ugly for his own father to want him dead. I mean, who would kill their own flesh and blood?"

A shout interrupted. "My lord." Standing a respectful distance away a teenage boy in palace livery bowed. "My lord, the king sent me. The council is about to begin."

"I'm on my way." Reluctantly Apsyrtus raised himself to his feet. "My quiet hour," he sighed. "You're lucky you don't have to go to these things. You should hear how those old graybeards drone on. I just hope I can stay awake."

Medea rose now too and brushed off the back of her brother's tunic. "Think about your bridal choices."

"Don't remind me." He surveyed the wall with its malevolent creepers. "You know, if you must persist in acting like one of the gardeners, why don't you at least grow something useful back here—like an aphrodisiac, for instance."

"I already have."

He looked skeptical. "Oh? Does it raise a man's ... interest?"

"Yes."

"Really?"

"Yes. Right before he croaks."

Apsyrtus smiled wryly, shook his head. "You're a witch, Medea."

II
Feast of Ares

GATHERING UP HER TOOLS, Medea made her way back to the stables where an old, white-haired servant was just leading her stallion into the yard.

"He's prickly today, my lady," the old man said, patting the horse's neck, "but Nutty's always a measure prickly, isn't he? Don't know how you handle him." He took the basket from her hands and gave her the reins. "Going up on the ridge are you, my lady?"

"Yes."

"Nice up there. Been there myself years ago. See for miles out to sea, can't you?"

"Yes, on a clear day."

"Well, it's clear now, but the wind's rising," he added, glancing up at the sky. "You'll come down, won't you, my lady, if it begins to get fierce?"

"I will."

He slung her cloak and a string of dried figs over the horse's neck. "Brought you a snack, my lady, in case you get hungry."

"Thank you."

Bowing, the servant left her and disappeared into the stable.

Medea pulled a fig off the string and held it on her upturned palm. The stallion bent to pluck it from her hand. As Medea watched him chew, her thoughts floated back to another time, fifteen years past, and a red-haired man.

* * *

Phrixus had been a citizen of the great world outside of Colchis, a free spirit who went where he pleased, did what he liked, felt at home in any company. Words came easily to him, and although a man of plain features, his red beard masking a homely face, Phrixus was the most attractive figure about the court. A refreshing presence in the altogether too solemn palace, he was a born raconteur and inveterate liar, these attributes adding to his charm. The cock-and-bull story about the fleece was typical of him.

To hear Phrixus tell it, he had been saved from death by a flying golden ram that whisked him from Greece all the way across the Black Sea to Colchis. Alighting on the shore he sacrificed the ram to Zeus and skinned it, preserving its wondrous golden fleece. Leaving aside the implausible marvels and the churlish ingratitude toward the very beast that rescued him, the most preposterous part of the story was that Phrixus would have slaughtered a full-grown ram. It was well known that he was squeamish at the sight of blood. Besides, anyone who examined the fleece closely could discern that there was nothing miraculous about it, nor had it been removed hastily by an amateur. Carefully cut and cleaned, the leather had been worked to a fine suppleness by a skilled practitioner of the art. Then, for reasons unknown, the thick wool had been brushed with pure, molten gold.

The king was dazzled by the fleece. Asking few questions about its origin, he offered Phrixus marriage to his elder daughter, Chalciope, in exchange for it. So at a stroke Phrixus purchased his welcome, admission into the royal family, and a social rank equal to anyone in Colchis. Yet he never won the king's trust. That Phrixus was a foreigner—a Greek, in fact—made him suspect. That he was carefree and irreverent only deepened the king's rancor. Nor was Phrixus's marriage without strife. Chalciope bore him four children, all boys, whom she doted upon, but she grew more and more jealous of her husband and his attentions to others. Then Phrixus died.

He was just forty-two, had gone to bed one night complaining of stomach cramps, and the next morning he was dead. The physicians said he had eaten something bad. His friends hinted that he had been poisoned. Death came early to many in those days, and from many unexplained causes. Yet Phrixus had seemed in the prime of life. At the Feast of Ares barely a week before, he had been carousing all over town, entertaining his adopted countrymen with his stories. The holiday was observed with huge bonfires ignited as soon as the sun went down. Throughout the city there was drinking and laughter, dancing and singing well into the night.

His custom was to pay each bonfire a visit in turn, stopping long enough to fill his cup and regale the giddy assembly with some improbable fiction. During his rounds that evening Phrixus paused at a crackling blaze near the palace and noticed his wife's twelve-year-old sister, Medea, standing in the shadows. The whisper around the city was that her mind was tainted, and the royal family rarely allowed her to be seen in public. In all the excitement she must have eluded the servants and slipped out. As the lurid silhouettes danced before the fire, Phrixus approached the slight figure, who sank deeper into the gloom of the palace wall.

"What are you doing here?" he asked quietly.

Medea said nothing.

"It's late," he told her. "You should be in bed."

The two stood silent in the darkness, their faces lit only by the leaping flames. Phrixus leaned closer and inhaled the natural perfume of the girl's skin. Slowly, tentatively, he raised his hand and stroked her hair, twirling one of her black locks gently in his fingers. He caressed the smooth skin of her neck, her shoulder. Meeting no resistance he was emboldened.

Kissing her full on the mouth, he sucked her breath deep into his lungs. He felt for the buds of her breasts beneath the thin fabric of her chiton, then down to the hollow of her belly. Just as he slid his fingers to her tender cleft, he suddenly let out a cry. Medea had thrust her hand beneath his tunic.

Her grip was firm as she squeezed the stiff thing in her grasp. Frozen and terrified, Phrixus gaped at the girl, but Medea's cool crossed eyes revealed only a remote curiosity, as if she were viewing some peculiar phenomenon. She tugged him, hard, and so roughly that it took his breath away, but it also aroused him to the point of madness. He moaned, and she tugged again, chafing and inflaming him, on the knife-edge between pain and ecstasy. Unable to resist, Phrixus jerked several times, then shuddered, his eyes rolling back into his skull. A thick, warm fluid spilled over the girl's knuckles. She relaxed her grip, and Phrixus collapsed against the wall.

In the glow of the firelight he stared stupidly as Medea withdrew her hand and examined the sticky substance clinging to it.

"Your children," she said evenly, then wiped it off on the sash of her gown.

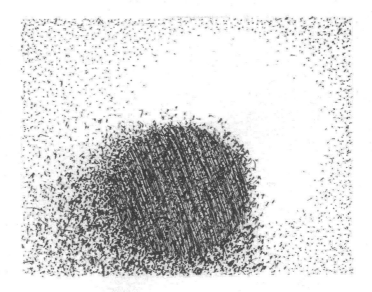

III
Caucasian Nymph

THE KINGDOM OF COLCHIS lay at the far eastern shore of the Black Sea. Then as now the climate was mild for its latitude. The River Phasis rose high up in the Caucasus Mountains and flowed through the fertile heart of the country before emptying its muddy contents into the sea near the capital, Aea.

Legend had it that Aea was built on the very hilltop where the god Helius stabled his horses, the fiery steeds that pull the sun across the heavens, but in fact the city was older than Helius. Some of the stones making up its wall had been pried laboriously from the earth a thousand years before by people of a different race, who spoke a different tongue, and who worshiped gods long dead and forgotten. Above the maze of narrow, unpaved streets crowded with low wooden structures, the palace stood upon a high plateau. A lopsided ring of stone buildings surrounded a central courtyard and fountain where a life-size bronze bull raged, a jet of water perpetually issuing from its mouth.

Apsyrtus did not stop to admire this bovine statuary as he

hurried past it to the main audience chamber, but he did pause at the entrance long enough to smooth down his hair and straighten his tunic. Then he nodded to the guards, who swung open the double doors. Before he was fairly across the threshold, a voice bellowed to him from within.

"Did you know where they were going?"

His father was standing at the head of the long table where a dozen councilors were now gazing at the startled young man.

"Well, did you or didn't you?" the king demanded.

"I'm sorry, my lord. Did I what?"

"Did you know where they were going?" the king repeated more insistently.

"Who, my lord?"

"Your nephews, damn it! Cytisorus. Argeus. Phrontis. Melanion." The recitation of each new name seemed to swell his anger the more. "Do you know where they are?"

"Hunting. They're on a hunting trip … aren't they?"

The king slumped back into his chair. "They've gone to Greece," he said with finality.

King Aeëtes was a gaunt, craggy-faced man. He dressed without ostentation except for a plain gold crown that circled his temples. This he now snatched from his head and dropped unceremoniously on the table in front of him. It made a small tinny clang as it fell.

Apsyrtus drew breath to speak again, but a gray-haired man seated next to the prince's empty chair put his finger to his lips and motioned for him to sit down. The king glared across the table at a straight-backed figure in military garb. "Can we stop them, Rhodus?"

"Even with unfavorable winds they would reach Beotia before we could catch up with them."

"And what about Beotia?"

"By all reports, they have one of the largest armies in Greece. If Cytisorus commands it, there's no point in our following them."

"So you propose we just sit here and do nothing!"

The councilors stirred uncomfortably, glancing one to

Richard Matturro

another. Finally, the gray-haired man said quietly, "That may be the best course to follow, my lord. Colchis is strong. We can protect ourselves if it comes to that, but I doubt it will. There is a good chance we will never see those four boys again. I suggest we wait."

Aeëtes frowned at each face around the table in turn. "All right, damn it. We'll wait."

There was an audible sigh of relief.

"But in the meantime," he continued, his voice rising, "I want the harbor guard doubled."

Rhodus sat up stiffly. "Yes, Sir."

"And I want a report on every foreign ship approaching or departing."

"Yes, Sir."

"And on every group coming overland."

"It will be done, Sir."

"And no one—including members of my own family," he added, sternly eying Apsyrtus, "no one is to leave without my permission." The king sat a moment longer, his face stony. Then abruptly he stood. "No more business today."

On their feet now too, the councilors bowed as he strode from the room. Then they turned to the prince who nodded their release. In knots of two or three they shuffled out, leaving only Apsyrtus and the gray-haired man behind.

"What the hell was that all about, Augeias?"

With some effort, Augeias lowered himself once more into his seat. "Apparently your nephews didn't go hunting."

"How do you know?"

"They were supposed to be back by now. When their mother questioned one of the servants, she became suspicious about the answers he gave. Under threat of torture, the servant confessed that the boys had really gone to their father's homeland. She came to the king in tears this morning with the news."

"But why would they go to Greece?"

"According to the servant, they'd got word that Phrixus's father had died. That means Cytisorus, being Phrixus's eldest, can claim the throne of Beotia."

Apsyrtus reached over for the crown that his father had dropped. "But I still don't see why everyone's so upset."

"You know how suspicious the king's always been of them. He thinks that once Cytisorus and his brothers are in possession of their Greek throne, they'll return to Colchis with an army and claim the succession here as well—your succession, my boy."

Apsyrtus was appalled at the idea. "No! Cytisorus wouldn't do that. I know him. He's no traitor. You don't think he's a traitor, do you, Augeias?"

Augeias shrugged his shoulders, his attitude noncommittal.

"Anyway, I'm Father's only son. That makes me the rightful heir. No one can dispute that."

"You can dispute anything you want when you've got an army at your back. Your sister Chalciope was the daughter of the king's first wife. Cytisorus could claim that since he's her eldest son, he takes precedence over you, who were born of the second wife."

"But that's ridiculous. That's not how succession works."

"People have used slighter claims."

Apsyrtus pushed back his chair and stepped to the window. In the courtyard below, Rhodus was barking orders to a small company of soldiers. Unconsciously the prince twisted the crown in his hands. "Cytisorus and I grew up together. He's only six years younger than I am. He's more like a brother than a nephew. He always accepted that I was next in line."

"Did he?"

"Of course. And he never even mentioned the king's first wife. That would have been his grandmother, right?"

"Yes." Augeias smiled slightly in remembrance. "It seems odd to call the poor girl a grandmother, she died so young."

There was a strange wistfulness in the old man's voice. Apsyrtus turned from the window. "Did you know her?"

"Oh, yes, I knew her. Asterodeia. Her name meant 'star goddess.' She was like one of the Immortals too. Beautiful, graceful, goodness itself. She was from the Caucasus, and your father used to call her his Caucasian nymph."

Richard Matturro

"He called her that?"

"Oh, your father wasn't always so grim. He was quite in love with her. Don't get me wrong; he loves your mother too. But Asterodeia was his first love, the love of his youth, and there's a difference."

"He never mentions her. No one ever does. What was she like?"

"She looked like your unfortunate sister Medea, but unlike her she was a happy creature. And she made the king happy too." He sighed. "Your father probably still grieves for her. It's bad enough that she had to die young, but worse that she died in childbirth. I don't think he's ever quite forgiven Medea for that."

"That was hardly Medea's fault."

"No, of course not. But there seemed to be no reason for it. She'd had no trouble with her first child, Chalciope. For some reason, though, only minutes after giving birth to Medea, Asterodeia just closed her eyes and died. It was very sad. Your father went up into his rooms and didn't come out for eight days. We feared for his life. And even after he emerged, he was in such anguish that I honestly thought he might never marry again. That was his inclination, I'm sure. But within a few months he chose Eidyia."

"What made him change his mind?"

"Your father is a good man, and he has a strong sense of duty. He knew the kingdom needed a male heir. Hence, he swallowed his grief and did what he had to do. You were born less than a year after the wedding. So you can see why he's not about to let Phrixus's sons come between you and the crown."

Apsyrtus regarded the bright coronet in his grasp. "I still think he's wrong about them. Those four boys aren't traitors. I know them better than anybody, and they've never lied to me."

"Until now," Augeias submitted.

The prince looked at him.

"They told you they were going hunting."

IV
Clashing Rocks

THE SEA STRETCHED so far into the distance that it blended imperceptibly with the sky in a hazy blue infinity. Only the gods could live beyond that invisible horizon, but not her gods. They inhabited a different place, closer, shadowy.

Medea dismounted. The outcropping in the foothills of the Caucasus provided a sweeping westward view. Glancing up she spotted a pair of hawks soaring overhead. In a long, graceful swoop the female landed on a dark mass hidden in a treetop farther down the ridge. Two tiny heads immediately popped up from the nest, their upturned, gaping maws silhouetted against the morning sky. The mother fed one, then the other, poking her own beak far down into theirs. She flew off again.

The string of figs in her hand, Medea sat beneath a twisted oak at the edge of the clearing. What had her brother said? She could get married if she really wanted to, if she were willing to act like everybody else. Inwardly Medea scoffed. She desired no wedded bliss. Marriage, children, family: they held no allure. In a world of overvalued baubles like the Golden Fleece, she had found the one true treasure—her own freedom. No one was going to take that away from her. She bit into a fig.

The wind was picking up noticeably. Out at sea, fishing boats headed toward shore. She watched as they maneuvered around two irregular boulders that rose up out of the water and towered forty feet in the air. Like a pair of rough sentinels the Clashing Rocks stood directly in the approach to the harbor. The god Ares was said to have set them there to protect Colchis from invasion. Unwary ships that tried to sail between would be crushed when the great monoliths suddenly collided. Of course, no one alive had ever seen the rocks move, nor did they provide any real defense, since vessels could sail around them with only minimal inconvenience. Nevertheless, the forbidden passage was notorious, and sailors of all nations stayed clear.

Still gazing westward, Medea noticed an unfamiliar craft some distance out in the open water. Foreign barks were not rare, for Colchis carried on a lively trade with other countries, but this wasn't a merchant vessel. Its sleek lines and formidable banks of oars suggested a warship.

Wind howled in the trees along the ridge, whipping the foliage into a loud fury, and out at sea the approaching ship took a battering. With its sails still unfurled, the vessel tilted perilously as it traveled at breakneck speed toward the harbor, the Clashing Rocks directly in its path. Medea scrambled to her feet, dropping the string of figs. The stranger craft plowed forward, entering the dreaded channel, its wide belly squarely between the great pillars. Would the stones move? *Could* they move? But no, it was just a legend. Still, was it not tempting fate to defy such an ancient tradition? Might not the gods punish such arrogance?

A moment passed, another, and the rocks stood motionless as they had stood for ten thousand years. Just as the stern slipped past into the calm security of the harbor, there was a horrifying screech louder than the gale. Medea's eyes snapped upward. The male hawk fluttered in the air, its pointed talons clutching the limp body of a mouse, but the nest was nowhere to be seen. The limb on which it had balanced was gone, shattered by the wind. To the roar of the elements the desolate bird added its own hideous shriek. Unmoved, the female sat on a nearby branch, tranquil amidst the fury.

* * *

Word spreading quickly through Aea that the curse had been broken, citizens rushed to the shore and stared in wonder at the ship as it glided majestically into the harbor. A grand, fifty-oared schooner, with two masts and two billowing sails, the prow cut the blue-green sea like a knife-edge, its wake nearly swamping the smaller craft nearby. The Queen of Heaven herself, Hera, was the figurehead, and the stern was carved in the likeness of a bird's fanning tail.

Impressive though the ship might be, it was the crew that now drew the crowd's excited attention. Their skin was red from the sun and sleeked with sweat, but these were not slaves. Tall and muscular, armed with bronze, they were attired like princes or the sons of nobility. When the ship touched the bank, several leapt over the side to pull it ashore and prop it up with poles. Directing their work was a well-favored youth with a light complexion and curly black hair. Though he seemed in charge, the mildness of his commands and his almost apologetic tone in uttering them did not display unequivocal rule.

While the crew secured the ship, four young men who were no strangers to the city alighted, causing a buzz among the spectators. Promptly a contingent of soldiers, spears at the ready, pushed their way through the gawking crowd toward the ship. Catching sight of them, the crew stopped what they were doing and drew their swords. In the margin of sand between the armed groups stood the curly-haired foreigner and the quartet of young men.

Rhodus stepped forward from the soldiers. "Cytisorus," he intoned carefully, "I must ask you what you mean here?"

"What do I mean?" the eldest of the four echoed. "Since when do I have to answer to you, Rhodus?"

"The king knows that you and your brothers went to Greece."

"What of it?"

"Who are these men?"

Their apparent leader stepped forward eagerly. "I think I can explain." His tone cheerful, his speech was that of mainland Greece.

"No one asked you," Rhodus broke in. He turned his attention to Cytisorus again. "The king wants to see you."

"I'll see the king when I'm good and ready."

"You'll see him now!"

The soldiers leveled their spears. The crewmen lifted their swords.

Looking nervously from one group to the other, the curly-haired young man forced a smile to hide his panic. "Please don't get the wrong idea, General. We have every intention of going along with you to see the king. After all, that's why we came all this way." He turned now to his own men and raised both hands, motioning for them to sheath their weapons. They made no move to obey him.

Over his shoulder he grinned at the mirthless Rhodus, then looked pleadingly to Telamon, the largest and most formidable of his followers, and mouthed the word, *"Please."* Telamon glared at the soldiers for a moment. Unhurried, he pulled himself up to his full height and nodded to his comrades. They lowered their swords.

The young man breathed a sigh of relief and turned back to Rhodus. "That's better. Now we can talk."

"Who the hell are you?" Rhodus demanded.

"Me? You're kidding, right? You mean you really don't know?" He pointed toward the harbor. "Didn't you see me go through the Clashing Rocks?"

Rhodus fixed him with an icy stare.

Ignoring the soldiers and their weapons, he crossed in front of them to his vessel and laid his hand lovingly upon gunwale. "Why, this is the famous ship *Argo*," he announced. "And I'm ... Jason!"

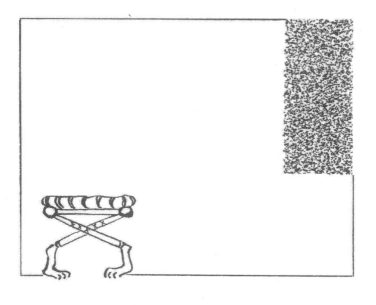

V
Quest

THE AUDIENCE CHAMBER had been hastily prepared and the upper ranks of Colchian nobility summoned. For the second time today the king entered the hall, but now accompanied by the queen, Eidyia, the prince, Apsyrtus, and the princess, Chalciope. In marked contrast to the controlled bearing of the others, Chalciope was visibly distraught, her matronly form quaking and her hands in constant motion twisting a small cloth. She took her seat at the edge of the platform next to an empty chair. This last place was reserved for the king's younger daughter, a mere formality since Medea never graced the court with her presence.

Without ceremony King Aeëtes nodded to the guards, who swung open the great double doors and escorted in Jason and the four sons of Chalciope.

Cytisorus made a formal bow to the dais, which Aeëtes acknowledged with the rough inquiry, "Where have you been?"

Taken aback, Cytisorus hesitated. "I went to claim my father's throne in Beotia, my lord."

"Who gave you leave?" Aeëtes growled.

There was mounting anger in Cytisorus's voice. "A man doesn't need anyone's leave, my lord, to take what is rightfully his."

"Is that so? Well, the thing that is rightfully mine, Cytisorus, is your loyalty."

"Is my loyalty called into question, my lord?"

"You stole from the realm in secret, lied about where you were going, and now return with an armed band. Are these the actions of a loyal subject?"

Cytisorus clenched his teeth. "Are you calling me a traitor, my lord?"

"*Are* you a traitor?" the king shot back.

Able to contain herself no longer Chalciope was on her feet. "Please, my lord, let my boy explain. I'm sure he had a reason for what he did. He's not a traitor."

"I'll be the judge of that," Aeëtes snapped. "Sit down."

She obeyed, her hand automatically carrying the bit of cloth to her eyes.

The king glared at Cytisorus. "And did you get your father's throne?"

"No, my lord. We never made it to Greece. We were shipwrecked off Cape Sinope. And it's thanks to this gentleman," he said, turning to Jason, "that we were rescued."

Aeëtes looked Jason up and down. "So you're from Greece."

"Iolcus to be precise, Sire," Jason announced, obviously pleased to have gotten the floor. "You've heard of it, haven't you? It's on the Pagasaean Gulf between Thessaly and Magnesia. I was born in Iolcus, but I was raised on Mount Pelion. That's a little to the east on a peninsula that sticks out into—"

"Spare me the geography lesson, Greek," the king broke in. "I want to know what the hell you're doing in my harbor with a warship."

"Oh no, Sire. *Argo*'s not a warship. She was built for speed, not for battle—except maybe against the elements. And we've had our share of those on the way. Your weather here in the Black Sea sure has a good deal more personality than what I'm used to back in the Aegean."

Aeëtes narrowed his eyes. "Are you a genuine fool, or do you just play at being one?"

"Sire?"

"Will someone tell this idiot that I am not his sire."

There was a ripple of laughter around the hall.

"Oh, I'm sorry, Si—my lord. But in my country—"

"In your country, men aren't satisfied to stay at home where they belong."

"Too true, my lord," Jason responded good-naturedly.

Aeëtes' frown deepened. "Listen, Greek, you've come to my kingdom with fifty armed men. You've got no goods to trade, so I want to know who the hell you are and what the hell you want here."

"I was just getting to that, my lord. You see, I'm Jason ... the son of Aeson." He paused for a moment to let the significance of his identity register, but the king showed no reaction except a grim stare. "My father was heir to the throne of Iolcus, but my uncle Pelias usurped the crown and had him killed, which made *me* the rightful heir. That was over twenty years ago. So when I came of age, I decided to go back to Iolcus—"

"To claim what was rightfully yours," the king interjected, with a sidelong glance at Cytisorus.

"Exactly right, my lord," Jason continued. "Well, Pelias was surprised to see me, to say the least. I thought he might laugh me right out of the palace, but instead he agreed to resign the crown to me if I could accomplish a certain mission for him. Of course he never expected me to attempt it, but within weeks I started building the *Argo* and gathering a crew of the best men in Greece. When we were ready to launch, it was such a big event that even Pelias was obliged to take part. He performed the sacrifice and daubed the blood on the keel himself."

Aeëtes' patience was wearing thin. "What does all this have to do with why you're here?"

"Well, we had to reach Colchis to complete our mission."

"What mission?"

Jason smiled broadly, proudly. "To fetch the Golden Fleece!"

There were gasps from several quarters, followed immediately by a dead silence. Slowly Aeëtes rose from the throne, his eyes bulging. But as he drew breath to speak, there was a noise to the side of the platform. The small door to the royal apartments opened.

Her enigmatic gaze sweeping the room, Medea stood for a moment in the threshold. Then, seemingly oblivious to the eyes trained upon her, she mounted the platform and calmly took the seat next to her sister as if she had been doing it all her life.

His rage somewhat dampened by the intrusion, but his face as stony as ever, the king turned back to Jason. "I don't know who you are, Greek, nor do I care. You may have come here thinking that we're just ignorant outlanders. Perhaps that's what you consider us back in Greece. But if you thought you could make dupes of us and rob us of the fleece, you have made a grave miscalculation."

"Oh no, my lord, we never expected to get the fleece for nothing."

"You're not going to get it at all. The fleece isn't for sale."

"Of course not, my lord. It was never our intention to buy it."

"Then what was your intention?"

"To perform a service for you, my lord, one that's so valuable that in gratitude you would willingly give us the fleece."

"And what service could you possibly perform that would be worth such a reward?"

Jason glanced at Cytisorus. "Ridding you of the Scythians?"

A faint murmur spread around the hall.

"They are a problem for you, I've heard," Jason continued, his voice softer. "We could fight them for you. We could crush them so decisively that they would never bother you again."

"With fifty men."

"With fifty of the finest warriors in Greece."

The king eyed the stranger for several moments, an uneasy tension in the air. Finally he announced, "We will think on your proposal. In the meantime, consider yourself our guest here in the palace."

With that, Aeëtes descended the dais and departed the hall through the little side door. Startled as everyone else by the turn of events, the queen, the prince, and Chalciope quickly followed him. The nobility would then have departed also, except that one member of the royal family lingered behind. Medea's stare was fixed on the curly-haired stranger in the center of the room.

Grumbling quietly to each other, the nobles shifted impatiently, unsure how long the king's daft daughter would keep them cooling their heels here. After a short time, though, and at her own cue, Medea rose from her seat. She glanced around the assembly, then, almost as an afterthought, offered a slight nod, releasing them, before disappearing from the chamber.

As the crowd dispersed, Jason leaned over to Cytisorus. "Who is she?"

"The king's younger daughter, Medea."

"Nice looking girl."

"She's also crazy."

"Really?" Jason looked toward the small door. "So much the better."

* * *

Rhodus stood before Aeëtes in the king's private chamber. "It's preposterous, Sir. There are too many Scythians."

"I know it." Aeëtes sat down wearily.

"The Greek was just boasting, or lying, trying to make fools out of us, Sir. Fifty men! What could he do with fifty men?"

"Not much to trouble the Scythians," Aeëtes replied, "but he could make mischief enough here."

"If you think so, Sir, why not just order them to leave?"

"And if they refuse, Rhodus?"

"Refuse? How can they refuse, Sir? There are many more of us than there are of them."

"So you would advise that we fight them in that event," he concluded, glancing over at Augeias, his old councilor, who stood silently in the corner.

"If we have to, Sir."

The king sighed. "Leave us, Rhodus."

"But Sir—"

"Keep a close eye on the harbor," the king added. "We'll talk again tomorrow."

Rhodus gave a formal bow and left the room.

When they were alone, the king motioned with his finger for Augeias to sit, which the old man did with evident relief.

"Military men!" Aeëtes shook his head disgustedly. "All they see is numbers. More of us than there are of them! Brilliant! We've got an armed camp on our beach, the cream of Greek nobility, young men trained in arms and eager for adventure— any adventure—and Rhodus wants to fight! Damn fool doesn't consider the casualties to our side even if we defeated them. Not to mention the families back in Greece. Does he think they'll sit idly by after their sons have been slaughtered? In six months we'd see a damned flotilla in the harbor. Military men! Geniuses!"

The old councilor chuckled.

"What do *you* think, Augeias?"

"Well, I don't think this Jason came here to fight us, my lord, nor to fight the Scythians for that matter."

"What do you think he came here for?"

"I think he came—they all came really—for a lark, a quest for the famed Golden Fleece. They're young, my lord. They remind me of the way we used to be when we were that age—full of piss and vinegar, to hell with the consequences."

"That's what scares me. They've come on a lark, but if saner heads don't prevail, it could result in disaster—for them, for us, for everyone." He sighed again, then with both hands massaged the muscles of his calf, which seemed to ache more and more lately. "I feel old, Augeias. I wish the prince weren't so young."

"Apsyrtus is a good boy."

"Yes, he's a good boy, but that doesn't make a good king. He doesn't understand the subtlety of statecraft, and he's not ready to stand up to someone like Rhodus. If it was my son sitting here instead of me, and Rhodus had advised fighting, Apsyrtus might easily have given in to him."

"He'll learn, my lord. Give him time."

The king seemed unconvinced. He leaned back, his mind on something else. Quietly he said, "Did you see her in the chamber?"

Augeias smiled. "Yes, my lord."

"When she stood there in the doorway, for a moment I thought ..."

"I know, my lord. The resemblance is striking."

"It's her hair, I think," the king continued, his voice soft, distant. "That was the way *she* used to wear it. Never put it up, never tied it back. I used to scold her for that. I'd tell her it looked unseemly, unbecoming of a queen. She knew I was teasing." He sat in silence, then shook his head as if to dispel the thought. "But we have to do something about this Jason, son of Aeson. You know, if these damned Greeks are bent on fighting the damned Scythians, I'm inclined to let them. Maybe when they see what they're up against, they'll think better on their 'lark.' What do you say?"

"It's tempting, my lord. But if they manage a to pull off a victory, which they might do in a limited skirmish, and then come back and claim the fleece, what will you do?"

"I suppose we'll have to make clear exactly what would constitute a victory."

"But that's ambiguous at the best of times."

Aeëtes cast his councilor a sly smile as he reached down to massage his calf again. "The subtlety of statecraft, Augeias, the subtlety of statecraft."

VI
Golden Fleece

SHE COULDN'T SLEEP. Up before dawn, Medea passed through the silent palace and slipped outside. A few bright stars still twinkled in the heavens, but to the east the sky was streaked with red, putting in relief the rugged outline of the Caucasus in the distance. As she crossed the courtyard, the morning mists parted, spun briefly in smoky whirlpools around her ankles, then resumed their lazy ascent skyward. Outside a small stone building she bent over a wooden box and lifted the lid. There was scurrying within. Her hand darted down and seized a mole.

Though the sky was brightening in the yard, the shadowy one-room edifice with its low timbered ceiling seemed to resist the morning. There was no furniture, only an elevated stone slab in which a bowl-shaped depression had been chipped out and smoothed to form a basin. With her own flawed eyes Medea examined the blind creature squirming in her grasp while she stroked its fur. Then, holding it over the rim, she drew the bronze dagger up under its throat. Quietly she chanted, *"Hecate can heal.*

Hecate can harm. Hecate can breed. Hecate can blight." She clenched the knife. "Great Goddess of the Undergloom, receive this sacrifice!"

"Hello!"

The blade slipped, sliced her palm. Bright red drops fell onto the altar while the mole, unhurt, scurried across the stone slab, flopped upon the ground, and disappeared into the shadows. The dagger still in her grip, Medea whirled around and faced the intruder.

Jason had been smiling. When he saw the flashing blade and the maddened glare, he backed away. "Oh, I'm sorry, Princess. I didn't mean to startle you. I was up early, and when I saw you go by—" he spotted the blood. "Hey, you're hurt." Jason stepped toward her, but she raised the dagger menacingly.

Hesitating, Jason stared at the red gash. "For God's sake, Princess, do you want to bleed to death?"

Medea glanced down at her hand. Again Jason made a move toward her; again the dagger went up, again he halted. Finally he reached down and ripped a long strip of cloth from the hem of his tunic, leaving an unsightly ragged edge. He held it up for her to see as he slowly approached. "All right, Princess, I'm going to try to help you, so if you want to stab me, fine. Then we'll both bleed together."

The dagger still threatened, but this time Jason ignored it. "Sit down," he ordered, indicating the stone slab.

"It's an altar, you fool, not a bench."

Jason viewed the stone, taking note of the basin, stained now with Medea's blood. "All right then, sit on the floor if you'd prefer."

She complied, and he knelt beside her. At the first touch of his hand, she jerked away. Gently he took hold of her wrist, then carefully wrapped the cloth strip around her palm. After several turns, he ripped the free end into two narrower strips and tied them, securing the makeshift bandage. "There," he said. "Now apply some pressure with your other hand—if you can bear to put the knife down for a minute, that is."

Medea slipped the dagger back into her belt. As she pressed her injured hand, she winced.

"Yes, I know. It's going to hurt for a while, but you've got to stop the bleeding, so hold it tight. How did you manage to cut yourself, Princess?"

She said nothing.

"What were you doing in here?"

Again she remained silent.

Jason glanced around the interior of the small building. "What is this place anyway? Wait! Don't answer. Are you always this good at conversation, or are you trying extra hard today just to impress me?"

She intended to scowl at him. Instead, to her annoyed surprise she couldn't suppress a small grin, which did not escape his notice.

"Hey, that's better. You're much more beautiful that way. We haven't been properly introduced. I'm Jason."

"I know who you are."

"They tell me your name is Medea. That's a pretty name. It means wisdom, doesn't it?"

"If you know enough to know that, then you know very well that it means cunning."

Jason laughed. "Well, we've established one thing. You're someone who won't be flattered. Good. I like that. My name means—"

"Healer."

"Yes! Kind of appropriate, don't you think?" He gestured to her bandaged hand. "Maybe I should have been a physician."

"But it's more profitable being an adventurer."

"Is that what you think? You're wrong. I only came on this quest because I had to." He paused. "Do you ride, Princess?"

"What business is that of yours?"

"I thought we might ride together. I'd like to see some of Colchis while I'm here."

"And you expect me to show you around?"

"Well, if you want to know the truth, you're the most interesting person I've met since I arrived."

"You're a liar. What do you want?"

Jason studied her features. Then he smiled and shrugged. "The fleece, of course."

"And you think I can help you get it."

"Can you?"

Without a word Medea rose and dusted herself off.

"Well, no harm in asking, right? I'd settle for a peek at it though. Can you at least show it to me?"

"Why should I?"

"For one thing, I saved you from bleeding to death."

* * *

The two guards at the Temple of Ares had retreated to the shade of the portico, but when they saw the approach of the princess and the Greek, they scrambled to stiff attention. "Good morning, my lady," one said mechanically as Medea and Jason passed between them.

Even in the dim light of the interior, Jason could make out the battle trophies adorning the walls, but it was the towering figure in the center that dominated the chamber. A huge wooden statue of a warrior in battle stance loomed over his head. With a stout trunk, a thick, round shield thrown before him, and holding a wide sword, the figure leered out from a square, lifeless face.

Jason stared up at the grim visage. "My God, he's ugly! Is this supposed to be Ares? I know he's the god of war and all, but in Greece we think of him as sort of a buffoon. No offense," he added, glancing now at Medea, "but you're the only country I know of that considers him a patron god."

"He's not *my* patron."

"Well, that's a relief. There's a statue of Hera back home like this, just terrible. No grace, no elegance, arms like a peasant, legs like tree trunks, and a face that could curdle milk. If you believe that likeness, you'd wonder what Zeus ever saw in her. I don't think there are three good sculptors in Greece. We had to go all the way to Mycenae to get someone to carve Hera on the *Argo*."

"And why Hera?"

Jason grinned proudly. "I'm her favorite."

"Is that so?"

"You don't believe me. I can see it in your face, but she came to me once. Not in her own form, of course." He stepped around to the side of the great statue, taking in its severe profile. "I had to ford a river, and on the bank was an old crone waiting to cross. Figuring I'd do a good deed, I offered to carry her, piggyback fashion. Well, she may have looked like a frail little lady, ninety pounds tops, but when she climbs on, Zeus be my witness, she's heavy as a small horse. So I hefted her up and somehow managed to stagger to the other side, though I lost a sandal in the process. Anyway, just before she slips down from my back she whispers in my ear, 'You're to be king.' I didn't think much of it. After all, she was ancient and maybe missing a few arrows in her quiver, if you know what I mean. Finding my sandal seemed more important at the time. I waded into the water again, but when I glanced over my shoulder, she'd vanished."

"So you assume that was Hera, and she protects you now."

Jason winked at her. "How else did I get through the Clashing Rocks?" He peered around, taking in the clusters of armaments on the walls. "So, where is it?"

At the rear of the temple was a small antechamber, the glow from a half-dozen sconces bleeding into the larger room. Jason stepped inside. Suspended from the ceiling like a gold curtain, the dazzling form reflected the torchlight, creating a perpetual aurora of light, color, and movement that danced across the walls.

"My God!" Jason gasped.

He moved toward the luminous shape, hesitated, then gingerly touched its gilded fibers. A tingle ran up his spine. "I was afraid it might just be a legend, but here it is, just like they described it. No, better! Much better!" Slowly he circled around it, unable to tear his eyes away. "All the while aboard ship I tried to imagine it. Look at the way it shines! Like a golden sun! I can't believe the king posts only two guards."

He turned to the doorway where Medea had been standing, but now she was gone. After a final glimpse of the fleece, he rushed from the chamber and caught up with her at the temple entrance. "Where are you going?" he said, grasping her arm.

She froze, her eyes fixed on his hand. "Let go of me."

"Oh, sorry, Princess." He relaxed his grip. "Forgive me. I just didn't want you to run off. I got absorbed in there. You have to understand, I traveled a thousand miles to see the Golden Fleece."

"Now you've seen it."

"I was still hoping we could take that ride together—if you'd be willing to lend me a horse, that is."

She said nothing.

"Listen, I know you don't trust me. After all, I'm one of those lying Greeks that your father's warned about."

"My father's views are not mine."

"Well, that's the first encouraging thing you've said to me. Does that mean you'll ride with me?"

Medea knew she should say no. She almost did say no. Then to her own surprise she found herself leading him to the stables.

VII
Circe's Grove

A KNOCK ON THE DOOR woke Apsyrtus with a start. As he sat
up sleepily, Eidyia strode into the room. He threw the bedclothes
over himself. "God, Mother, can't you at least wait until I let you
in?"

"I know what you look like." Tall, with intelligent eyes, Eidyia
was a handsome woman of forty-five. She bore herself with the
dignity required of her position, but none of the haughtiness that
sometimes accompanies aristocratic rank. "You should be up by
now," she chided. "I need to talk to you."

The prince yawned, then shoved over to make room for her to
sit on the edge of the bed. "What do you want to talk about?"

"First of all, your nephews."

"Don't tell me you think Cytisorus is after my crown too."

"I'm not sure. I may not have thought so a month ago, but
when something very precious suddenly comes within reach,
people change. He's under the influence of this clever Greek now,
and one or the other of them may conclude that the throne of

Colchis is up for grabs." She was silent for a moment. "Cytisorus has three brothers, you know. You have none."

"So what?"

"You have no one you can absolutely depend on, no real allies."

"What are you talking about? I have the council, the army. They're both loyal."

"They're loyal enough to the king, but should there be a sudden change in government, they'll be just as loyal to the next king, whoever he is. If Cytisorus mounts a strong enough challenge to the succession, they may not lift a finger to help you." She looked him dead in the eye. "Apsyrtus, you're my only child. It was never my ambition to marry a king, nor to bear a son who'd be a king. And none of this would have happened if your father's first wife had lived. Maybe the gods had a hand in it, or maybe it was just a series of accidents that brought us to this point. In any case, as the world stands now, it's your right to be the next king, and if I were you, I'd be damned if I'd let anyone usurp that right."

The prince stared at her. He'd never heard his mother speak this way before.

"You may not be able to change who you are," she continued, "but if you want to succeed your father, you're going to have to change how people think of you."

"Father never cares what people think."

"Don't be taken in, Apsyrtus. Affecting not to care is part of his design. People may not like him, but they've come to respect him over the years, and they think he's a good king. They don't know what to think of you."

Her son began to protest, but she shut her eyes and shook her head to silence him.

"You show no interest in government. You lie in bed until noon, then spend your day in idleness. You take no pains to impress anyone with the strength of your mind or your character. Make no mistake: you're effectively tossing your father's crown in the air. When it falls, it could land right on Cytisorus's head. And keep in mind, once in power he won't be able to let the legitimate heir survive."

He shifted uneasily.

Eidyia rose, smoothed the linen where she had sat. At the door she turned to him again. "Your unfortunate sister Medea acts contrary to her own best interest because her wits are flawed, but in your case, Apsyrtus, there's no excuse."

* * *

A stand of ancient willows grew along the bank, their pendulous boughs raking the muddy water of the River Phasis. The road from the city diverged here, a narrow path winding its way into the thick wood. Though high noon outside, Jason felt a hushed, unnatural twilight close in around them as they entered the forest. He eyed the gnarled old trunks hidden from the sun by the impenetrable canopy of shifting, rustling leaves.

"Gloomy place," he muttered. "Does it have a name?"

Up ahead Medea plucked a hawthorn berry, split it with her thumbnail, and sniffed the juice. "Circe's Grove."

The deeper they went into the wood, the more skittish Jason's mare became, picking her way gingerly along the trail. He leaned to stroke her neck and calm her, but suddenly there was a loud crack. The mare flung her head up wildly and leapt aside nearly throwing Jason to the ground.

"What the hell was that?" He quieted the beast, then dismounted to investigate. On the trail a large bone lay splintered, broken by the mare's hoof. Jason lifted the two pieces and fitted them back together. A femur, the thighbone, but from what animal? Too short for a horse, too long for a fox or a dog. He scanned the ground. The forest floor was littered with bones, all chalky gray and pockmarked. He recognized a clavicle, several vertebrae, and—

"My God, it's a skull. They're human!" He dropped the fragments in horror. "Where did they come from?"

"They fall from the trees." Medea slipped down from her horse and tied it next to Jason's. "Would you like something to eat?"

"The trees?!" Jason looked skyward. Fifty feet above his head a tattered, shapeless fabric flapped in the summer breeze. Not far away, suspended from another limb, a bulging cylindrical shape swung heavily like a hammock. The treetops were full of these grotesque bundles, all in various stages of decay.

"What were they, criminals?" he cried. "Is this the way you execute them? String them up alive and expose them?"

"Will it be easier for you to steal the fleece if you think of us as barbarians?" Medea sat beneath one of the willows. "It's our funeral custom. Women are buried. Men are wrapped in animal hides and tied in the tree branches. When the flesh is consumed and the hide rots, the bones fall back to earth."

Incredulous, Jason stared up into the trees again. "Queer custom!" He shuddered. Having suddenly lost his appetite, he refused the cheese she offered, but he took a long pull on the wineskin before sitting down next to her.

Medea asked, "What do you do with the dead in your country?"

"We bury them."

"All of them?"

"Yes, of course."

"Even famous warriors?"

"Well, no," Jason conceded. "They're burned on a funeral pyre."

"What's that?"

"It's a wooden platform, six or eight feet high—higher if it's a particularly important person. Along with the body we pile on some of his possessions, maybe trophies he's won, his armor maybe, locks of his wife's hair, tributes from his children, that sort of thing. Then his friends and family gather round, and the whole thing is set afire."

"I see." She raised her chin slightly, as if pondering this. "Queer custom."

"All right," he snickered, "you're cunning, like your name. You knew very well what a funeral pyre is." He reached for the round of cheese, hesitated, then broke off a piece for himself. "Hell of a place for a picnic. Why is it called Circe's Grove?"

"Circe was my aunt. She was a votaress of Hecate, and she would take me here to gather herbs. She taught me about plants and animals."

"Did she teach you about people?"

"Enough to know when I'm being mocked."

"So, what happened to Aunt Circe? Did she die?"

"She may as well have. She went to Aeaea."

"Aeaea. Never heard of it. I have heard of Hecate though. She's the goddess of crossroads or something like that."

Medea turned away, her voice distant. "She's the goddess of unforeseen junctures in destiny. She dwells in the Underworld and infects the earth with noxious vines and poisonous fruit."

Jason stole a sideways glance at her. "Thank you for clarifying that. Most Greeks don't believe in her, you know."

"Then most Greeks are fools."

"Well, that may be so in any case," Jason responded. "If Hecate's the goddess of 'unforeseen junctures,' then maybe she's responsible for bringing us together, you and me."

"Hecate doesn't bring people together. She sets them at odds and sows discord."

"Then why would you want to worship a bitch like that?"

Medea turned on him with a sudden passion. "Don't speak of her that way!"

"Well, I didn't think—"

"You don't understand. She's very powerful. Make a libation, ask forgiveness, right now!"

"All right," he soothed, "I'll do it."

Jason pulled the stopper from the wineskin. Closing his eyes, he bowed his head respectfully, and Medea followed suit. "Lady Hecate," he intoned, "please forgive the words I spoke. I meant no offense. To your great honor and glory." He opened his eyes, spilled an ounce on the ground, then sipped. He passed the skin to Medea and watched her drink. "All right?" he asked tentatively.

Relieved, Medea inhaled deeply. After a few moments she said, "Tell me about your country."

"Greece? Oh, it's a beautiful place: mountains, broad plains, hillsides covered with olive groves, and everywhere within sight of the sea. I live in the Pagasaean Gulf, which is almost a complete circle, a hundred miles of white beaches enclosing a bay so blue it makes your heart ache."

"Who taught you how to talk like that?"

Jason lifted his shoulders. "Chiron, I guess. He was my tutor when I was growing up. He's dead now, long dead. He was seventy or seventy-five then—I don't think he knew for sure. And homely, with a face like a horse. People called him the Centaur. And it didn't help matters that he snorted all the time. There always seemed to be something troublesome about his nose. He walked hunched over, favored one leg, and had a rasping voice, but could that man talk! He was a poet too."

"Do you remember any of his poems?"

"Sure. You like poetry?"

"We have very little poetry in Colchis. Can you recite one for me?"

"I think so." Jason fell silent, recollecting the verse. He began:

> "Hot and dry young Actaeon was,
> And thirsty nigh to death.
> Since morning he had chased the stag,
> But now had stopped for breath.
>
> He leaned his bow against a tree,
> Allowed his dogs to rest,
> Then wandered in a shady wood,
> An uninvited guest.
>
> Anon a gentle stream he spied,
> That flowed from out a glade.
> It widened to a sheltered pool,
> And in the pool a maid.
>
> Of all fair maids the youth had seen,
> The fairest maid of all,

Then all at once made fairer still:
She let her mantle fall.

No ordinary girl was she,
Who bathed in forest pool.
She was the goddess Artemis,
The virgin and the cruel.

Actaeon should have turned his head,
But now was he enrapt.
For better view he took a step.
A brittle twig he snapped.

Enraged, the goddess scanned the wood,
Observed the spy so rash.
She dipped her hand into the pool,
The hidden youth to splash.

The droplets flew toward Actaeon,
And fell upon his side.
Four legs he grew, a coat of fur,
Great antlers tall and wide.

He bounded forth out of the wood.
His dogs picked up the scent.
They chased him, caught him, pulled him down.
The stag's poor heart they rent.

And in the forest Artemis,
Forgotten of her wrath,
Rinsed clean her soft and lovely limbs,
And finished with her bath."

Jason leaned back. "I can't believe it came back to me after all these years. What do you think?"

Medea said simply, "That was just … terrible."

Doubling over, Jason howled with laughter. "It was, wasn't it? Chiron was a miserable poet, but nobody dared tell him that! He churned out these cheesy rhymes by the bucketful." When settled down again, Jason looked at Medea. He found something compelling in those unfathomable crossed eyes, which now almost smiled at him, almost seemed human. "Your family doesn't really know you, do they? No one does. You're not crazy at all."

She handed him the wineskin. "Tell me more about Greece."

VIII
Stratagems

THIS WAS HIS FIRST VIEW of the *Argo*. Apsyrtus loved ships, and the stunning vessel, backlit by the setting sun, was larger and sleeker than anything he'd seen before. But the *Argo* was not the reason for his visit. He scanned the harbor. Greeks had fairly well taken over the waterfront, their tents dotting the shore, their gear strewn carelessly about the sand. Crewmen passed the time fishing or playing games on the beach. One tossed a disk with Cytisorus, who spied the prince.

"Over here, Unk!"

It was a half-serious form of address, pointing up the absurd closeness in their ages. Cytisorus sailed the disk one last time, then jogged over and clapped Apsyrtus on the shoulder. "I was wondering when the hell you'd come down. I knew you had to see the ship."

"Your brothers told me I'd find you here. They said you only come back to the palace to sleep."

"I don't feel too comfortable in the palace right now, if you know what I mean."

"You can't blame the king this time. You told everyone you were going on a hunting trip—me included."

"I'm sorry about that, Unk. If the king found out, he never would have let us go."

"He wouldn't have found out from me." The young man's eyes strayed to the *Argo*.

"Want to see her up-close?"

With obvious pride as if the craft were his own, Cytisorus led the prince aboard. He explained the rigging, showed him into the small cabin, led him down into the cool darkness of the hold. Apsyrtus stood at the helm briefly and imagined her underway, the wind in his hair, the prow smartly cutting the waves. Then he glanced around at the Greeks lounging about the deck. An arrogant lot, curt and ill-mannered, they ignored him as if he were a poor relation instead of a prince.

"Splendid ship," Apsyrtus remarked afterward as he strolled with his nephew up the beach, "but I can't say much for your new friends."

"They're not too fond of Colchians either. Remember, they didn't exactly get a warm reception when they arrived. Besides, they think of this place as a backwater, and frankly I agree with them."

Apsyrtus swallowed the insult and merely remarked, "When the *Argo* sails, you plan to hitch a ride to Greece?"

Cytisorus came to a stop. "How did you know?"

"It was an easy guess." The prince, halted now too, glanced back at the ship. "Jason's agreed to take you?"

He nodded. "You've got to understand, Unk: there's nothing for us here anymore. We're unwelcome in our own country. The king only wants us around so he can keep an eye on us." He lowered his voice. "Listen, I know your father doesn't like me, and you know I don't like him, but you and I have always been friends—since we were kids. You have a crown waiting for you here. Well, I have a crown waiting for me in Beotia. Can you really blame me for wanting to take it? I have to go there." He paused. "You're not going to tell him, are you?"

"I won't say anything, but what does Jason get out of this deal?"

His nephew hesitated.

"He expects to get the fleece," Apsyrtus concluded. "That's it, isn't it? Does he plan to steal it?"

Cytisorus bit his lip. "I don't know. He never said so, but—"

"But what?"

"They've come an awful long way to go home empty-handed."

* * *

"My lady? My lady? Are you all right?"

Medea's eyes popped open. Hovering over her was the familiar wrinkled face of her maid. "Yes, Ornis, what's the matter?"

"I didn't want to disturb you, my lady, but I was a mite worried. I've never known you to stay in bed this late. I was afeared you were sick."

"I … had trouble getting to sleep last night."

"What with all the commotion this morning, I was surprised it didn't wake you up."

"What commotion?"

"Oh, the king called that Greek to the court again, and of course every busybody in the palace had to show up. Lord High Zeus, you'd think it was God Almighty—"

"What happened?" Medea interrupted.

"Your father accepted his terms. He told them that if they defeat the Scythians good and proper, they can have the fleece. Not that there's any danger of that, my lady. Anyone foolish enough to fight the Scythians—"

Medea sat up, suddenly wide-awake. "The Greek—where is he?"

"Well, I don't rightly know, my lady. On his way back to his ship, I should think."

She bolted from the bed, nearly toppling Ornis.

"What is it, my lady? Can I get you something?"

"My horse."

* * *

He heard hoof-beats behind him. Alone and on foot, halfway down the dusty road from the city, Jason feared an ambush. He reached for his sword, then cursed when he remembered he'd purposely gone to the palace unarmed. Determined at least to confront his attacker head-on, he spun around.

Medea pulled her stallion to a halt.

"Princess!" He breathed deeply. "You had me scared there for a minute. What's the hurry?"

"Do you really plan to fight the Scythians?"

"Bad news travels fast."

"Fool! The king expects you to get killed."

"Then you'll be rid of me." He turned to continue on his way.

Medea swung down from her horse and grabbed his sleeve, jerking him to a stop. "You want the fleece. That's what you came here for. So if you get it, you can just leave, right?"

"I suppose that's right."

"Well, I'll get you the damned fleece."

"Why would you—?" But Jason didn't need to finish. To his stunned delight, the answer was there on her face, behind the stern mask. "You're worried about me. You're afraid I really might get killed."

"Don't flatter yourself."

"I'm not flattered. I'm touched. You don't understand, Princess. No one's ever cared about me before." And then he repeated, "No one," with a sincerity in his voice that Medea had not heard before. He looked up toward the city. "But what will become of you?"

"What do you mean?"

"If you help me get the fleece and I leave here, what will you do?"

"I'll do as I've always done."

"Go back to tending your garden—alone? Riding your horse in the hills—alone? Praying to your wicked goddess—alone?"

"What's that to you?" Her words were defiant, but the timbre hollow.

A thought started to form in Jason's mind, thrilling but terrifying.

"Come with me, Medea. Come back to Greece with me."

She stared at him.

"What kind of a life do you have here in Colchis? People treat you like you're an idiot."

"Yes, but at least here I'm a princess. In Greece I'd just be your whore."

"I'm not asking you to be my whore." Jason looked deep into her deformed but inexplicably appealing eyes. "I'm asking you to be my queen."

"You're crazy."

"Then we make a pair, don't we? Listen, Princess, I'm not married. You're not married. There's a throne waiting for me in Greece. Share it with me."

She tried to turn away, but he grasped her hand—her injured hand—and the wound stung her soul.

"Come with me, Medea."

"You don't know what you're saying."

"I do. You're the strangest, the most beguiling creature I've ever met. Your eyes are black as death. When you look at me, you scorch my skin. Come with me, Medea."

IX
Nightfall

Now what? Visits from two of the royal family in one evening? Most nights on guard duty he barely saw a soul from sunset to sunrise. Deimas whistled to his young companion, a new recruit, and pointed toward the figure approaching the temple. "We're popular tonight," he whispered.

"What do you suppose the nutty bitch wants?"

Deimas shook his head. "She's got two cups. Libations to Ares, I guess."

The younger man sniggered. "Maybe she'll ask him to straighten her eyes, or grow some decent tits on her flat chest."

"Quiet, you jackass! She'll hear you."

Medea climbed the steps with care so as not to spill the liquid.

"Good evening, my lady." Deimas nodded respectfully. "Come to pray, have you?"

She seemed nervous, hesitant. "No, I … brought you some wine."

The soldiers exchanged glances.

"It's a long night," she explained. "I thought you might be thirsty."

"Well, that's most kind of you, my lady!" Deimas took both cups from her and handed one to his companion. "Why, we're doubly honored tonight. As I was just saying to—"

"Please drink quickly," Medea interrupted, glancing over her shoulder.

It was good palace wine, not the swill they served in the barracks. Deimas would have preferred to savor it longer, but he promptly tossed it off. When they were both finished, Medea snatched the cups. In dismay Deimas watched her hurry down the steps and back toward the palace. "What the hell do you make of that?"

The younger man lifted his shoulders. "Like I said: nutty bitch."

"Three years I've pulled night duty here, and not once has she so much as shown her face. And now out of the blue she brings us wine!"

"Maybe she fancies you." The recruit yawned.

"Royals! Who can understand them?" Deimas shrugged. "Good wine, though. Damn good wine." He too yawned.

* * *

Under the palace wall, Jason and two of his men peered out into the darkness. "Why should we trust her?" Telamon demanded.

"It'll be all right," Jason assured him. "We can trust her."

The other man shifted uneasily. "How did you get her to do it?"

"I didn't, Peleus. It was her idea."

"It's a trap," Telamon declared. "We should get the hell out of here."

"Wait. She's coming."

Medea's slender form emerged from the shadows. Taking in Jason and the others, she steadied herself against the wall.

"How did it go?" Jason asked. "Did it work?"

She took a deep breath. "They'll be asleep for hours."

"Go get your things," he said, touching her shoulder tenderly. "We'll come back for you when we're done. Don't worry. Everything's going to be fine."

* * *

Apsyrtus didn't know why he was doing this. If he was afraid that the fleece might be stolen, on his own authority he could have appointed additional guards tonight. It was hardly necessary for the crown prince to stand sentry himself, but his mother's words kept echoing in his conscience. He needed to take *some* action, assume *some* responsibility. So he had strapped on his sword that had never been lifted in anger, hefted his shield that had never deflected a blow. Entering the temple thus armed, he'd caught one of the soldiers smirking.

That was hours ago, but there were still many hours before morning, and he sat at the base of the silent, glowering statue barely able to keep his eyes open. A fine sentinel he was! If the soldiers outside could see him, they would scorn him indeed. Maybe his mother was right. He wasn't ready, wasn't worthy to be king. Nor would this pointless vigil impress anyone. As usual, he had made the wrong choice, and thus made a fool of himself again, if only in his own eyes. For all the good he was doing, he might as well be back in his bed asleep.

He stood up to stretch his legs and throw off the drowsiness. As he walked aimlessly around the shadowed interior of the temple, he eyed the captured arms hung proudly on the walls. A dozen successful campaigns were represented here. Which people had used the long, double-barbed spear? Whose shield was painted with the boar's head? What warrior had worn the leather helmet studded with bronze? When Apsyrtus was a boy, his father had told him stories of these defeated enemies, but he'd taken no interest. Now he regretted his inattention.

At the rear of the temple Apsyrtus paused before the anteroom. Illuminated by flickering torchlight, the golden form shimmered quiet and alone. He stepped inside, hesitated, then slipped off his shield and leaned it against the wall. Relieved of the unaccustomed burden, he made a great circle with his arm to get the kinks out. The insignificant currents of air stirred the fleece ever so slightly, and the reflected light danced upon the walls in a shifting, mesmerizing pattern.

Oh, maybe things weren't quite so bleak after all, he thought, not quite so hopeless. He could learn to be a worthy successor to his father. If he made mistakes, well then he made mistakes, but damn it, he was determined to try.

There was a noise behind him, footsteps and shuffling. Spinning around, he was stunned to see three men now crowded into the small room.

Greeks! In a terrifying flash of recognition, Apsyrtus reached for his sword, but one of them was already upon him. He felt his breath knocked out, and didn't even know at first that he had been stabbed. It felt absurdly like an embrace. The Greek hugged him roughly with one arm, the other pushing into his gut and jerking upward. The pain reached his consciousness at the same instant as the obscene smell of his own entrails. He tried to scream, but a hard hand was locked over his mouth. Gagging on the blood that filled his throat, his nose, he struggled as his mind clouded. When the hands finally let him go, his knees buckled, and he collapsed upon the floor.

Apsyrtus felt the cool stone against his cheek. He squinted at something close to his face. Bright, shiny, and still unused, his shield reflected the golden glow of the fleece hovering above. He raised a finger to touch it, but then the shield disappeared, along with the pain, the Greeks, and the world.

* * *

"Oh my God," Jason cried, "it's the prince! You've killed the prince! It's her brother!"

"Let's do what we came to do," Telamon commanded. He motioned to Peleus.

Shocked at what had just happened, Jason stared dumbly at the lifeless body as the others lifted the fleece from its hooks, threw a piece of sailcloth over it, then heaved it onto their shoulders.

"Wait!" Frantically he pointed at Telamon's bloodstained tunic. "She can't see you like this. You've got to get rid of it."

"The hell I do!"

"*Listen to me!* She can't find out! Don't you understand? *Ever!* You take the fleece back to the ship. I'll stall a little while before bringing her down, but you've got to change before we get there."

Peleus grabbed Jason's arm. "We'll take care of it, but you'd better hurry. We have to push off tonight."

They bore the fleece from the chamber. Lingering, Jason glimpsed again the crumpled figure in the widening pool of blood. "I'm sorry," he whispered. "I'm so … sorry."

* * *

The floppy leather bag lay on her bed. Along with her clothes, her herbs and potions, it held her fears. Medea had never been farther from Aea than half a day's ride on horseback. Now she was about to leave everything she knew, everything familiar. Worse, once she left Colchis, she would be at Jason's mercy. Would it not be better to bar the door against such a man than to go with him? And yet, how empty, how bleak life would be if she could never see him again.

Medea fell to her knees. Hecate, the goddess of crossroads, must know what to do at this terrible juncture. Stay? Remain the mad princess whom everyone shunned, an outcast in her own land until the day she died? Or leave. Gamble on a new life in a new country as a new person. She begged the goddess for an answer, squeezed her eyes shut and prayed for a sign.

But there was no sign. In the cool darkness of that evening long ago no miracle occurred, no law of nature was violated. The waves of the Black Sea washed the shore as they always had, the gulls cried, and in a room in a palace in a city that would one day be dust, a young woman rose to her feet. She slung the leather bag over her shoulder, stood for a moment at the door, then passed silently into the night.

Richard Matturro

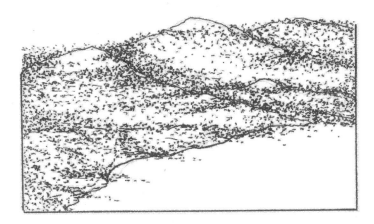

X
White Gown

HE HAD EXPECTED IT to be a lark, an adventure. Now an invisible harpy squatted on his shoulder, cackling at his simplicity. Crowns descend by blood, one way or another. Since morning Jason had haunted the stern, his eyes cast eastward, backward. He imagined the entire Colchian fleet in pursuit, half-anticipated it, fully deserved it, but the limitless waves receded in the distance, vacant and indifferent.

Peleus stood behind him. "The sun will be down in a few hours, Jason. We'll need supplies. There's a cove a couple of miles up the coast."

"All right. Put in for the night."

He'd given over the small cabin to Medea, and he hadn't seen her all day—dared not appear before her lest she read on his face what had happened the night before. The Golden Fleece lay on the deck, a grimy cloth thrown over it. He would willingly hurl the thing into the ocean if he could have heaved with it the guilt in his soul. Jason leaned on the gunwale and stared at the wake as he felt the *Argo* shift, veering toward shore.

The cove was well hidden from the sea by a thick grove of pines. While his crew made camp, Jason stole out to the beach and searched the open water once again. The horizon was still unbroken. Red streaks were piled rank upon rank in the evening sky, presided over by a thin sliver of moon. Below, breakers washed the barren coast.

"Don't worry," a voice said. "They won't follow." Medea was seated on a ledge just above him.

"You startled me." Jason hesitated, then looked out to sea again. "What makes you so sure?"

"My father won't go to war over a trinket."

"A trinket," Jason mused. "You'd be surprised what people will do for trinkets." He turned to her. "How are you doing?"

"I'm all right."

"Hungry?"

She shook her head.

"Are you sure? Mopsus is good with venison. He's a Lapith."

"A Lapith?"

"His tribe," Jason shrugged. "They pride themselves on their cooking."

"I know so little about your country."

"You'll learn." He climbed up and sat by her side. "That's where we're going," he said, pointing to the darkening sky in the west. "The sun rose in Colchis, and it will set in Greece."

"You have family there."

"Just my mother, in Mount Pelion. I have no brothers or sisters."

"She'll be worried about you."

"I doubt it. Mother's not a worrier. This expedition may have been my idea, but she financed it—with the last of my father's treasure."

Medea drew her knees up. "My family will figure out what I did, and they'll hate me, my brother most of all. I can never go home again."

Jason slipped his arm around her waist and pulled her close.

"Your home will be with me. We'll be married."

She was silent for several moments. "How do you marry in Greece?"

"You just declare it—in a public ceremony, usually—and then you have a party, where people drink and dance."

"And how do you un-marry?"

He snorted. "The same thing, but usually without the party."

"I never expected to be anyone's wife, never wanted to be."

"Well, that was before you met me."

She looked at him. "Where do I sleep tonight?"

"In my tent, of course."

"And where do you sleep?"

"Next to you if I'm lucky. If not, then next to Peleus in his tent, and I'll listen to him snore all night. What would you like?"

She turned toward the reddening sky. "I'd like some wine."

* * *

Outside the tent she could hear the gentle lap of the waves in the cove and voices of the men as they huddled around their fires eating dinner. Medea shivered slightly, lifted a blanket from the pallet and draped it over her shoulders. She was thinking of a little white gown. How old had she been? Six? Seven? To escape the servants, she'd crawled in the dust and cobwebs behind the amphorae in one of the palace cellars, but the two old women found her. They bundled her up to her bath, then dressed her, squirming, in the dainty chiton. Directly she was led into the great hall where her father waited, eager to present his family to the ambassador from Troy.

The royal emissary had been a large, imposing figure with thick arms and a shaggy beard. He smiled down condescendingly and leaned over to pat Medea's cheek. Without warning, she seized his hand and sank her teeth into his palm as the shocked assembly looked on. The ambassador let out a howl and tried to pull away, but she bit down all the harder. Attendants scurried to his aid and finally succeeded in prying her loose. Medea was carried out of the hall, blood dripping from her chin onto the white frock.

Now, clean and new, the gown was hanging within reach once more. She had but to slip it on. "If you'd just act like everybody else," Apsyrtus had said. Was he right? Was that the price of happiness? She thought of Jason, his curly black hair, his soothing voice, his rambling speech, the pleasure she felt just being near him. Were not these common joys the birthright of every human creature? And if so, why not hers as well?

The tent flap flew open, and Jason appeared with two bronze goblets. "Sorry I took so long. The cups were packed away. Without any women around, we generally drink right from the skins." Carefully he handed her one, then crossed his legs and settled on the pallet next to her. "It's from Lemnos. The wine, I mean. We stopped there on the way to Colchis. Hypsipyle, the queen, held a state dinner in our honor. You know what she told us? When Lemnians go to war, women fight right alongside the men. What do you think of that?"

"You assume women can't fight?"

"Well, I don't know. Maybe they can, but the only time I saw you draw your weapon, you managed to stab your own hand."

Medea giggled in spite of herself. "How do you do it? You make me laugh at my expense. No one's ever been able to do that."

"Everyone else was afraid of you. They saw someone who wanted to hide. I see a girl who wants to be found."

She felt naked. Lowering her eyes, she tasted the wine. After a moment, she asked, "How long before we get to your home?"

"A few weeks, depending on the weather. We'll go down to Attica first. Half the men are from the Peloponnese. Once we drop them off, we'll head east around Sunium, then north along the coast of Euboea until we reach Sciathos—" Jason suddenly broke off. "I'm sorry. None of this means anything to you."

"Are they all separate kingdoms?"

"Worse. Some are divided up into a dozen separate kingdoms. And they're forever squabbling about one thing or another. Chiron told me this gruesome story once about—"

Medea put a finger on his lips. "Not tonight, Jason."

Surprise and delight overspread his features. "You said my name! It's the first time I ever heard you say it."

"I've said it in my mind."

He put his arm around her. "I want to know you, Medea. Can I? Can I ever?"

"I don't know." She hesitated, then reached up and unfastened her broach. "But you can love me."

*　*　*

Jason's touch was tender, compelling, but it was her own name that lured her. "Medea." He whispered it over and over again like a conjuration. Her nails pinioned his back, her legs squeezed his life, yet he beckoned her: "Medea, Medea," calling her forth—but to what?

Afterward she lay by his side listening to the night birds and the fierce beating of her heart. Out of the darkness she heard him say quietly, "Marry me tomorrow, Medea. I don't want the men to think you're my whore for even one day."

Icy and snow-covered like the peaks of the Caucasus were the warnings, but in the valley rolled a gentle fog, lovely, insinuating, and out of it a voice called her name again and begged her to come out—to come out and be like everybody else. Softly, irresistibly, the mist rose until it shrouded even the highest promontory.

XI
Confidants

No one was inclined to dance at Jason's wedding. In a hasty ceremony on the beach the next morning, Jason declared before his men that he and Medea were husband and wife. Then, after a brief libation to solicit the gods' blessing, they pushed off. And so Medea spent her first month of married life on the very public, very male deck of the *Argo* as they sailed toward her new home. If some of the crew curbed their behavior in deference to her, others, who frowned on marriage with outlanders, conceded nothing at all, but Medea was unfazed. Their coarse language and boisterousness were eclipsed by the upheaval inside her. For Medea, the world had shifted.

She experienced an absurd pleasure simply in watching Jason. He shared a jest with Peleus, questioned Nauplius about the route, and she couldn't take her eyes off him. The next moment he would be at her side chattering about Greece, his arm thrown casually, affectionately over her shoulder, and she would find herself smiling for no reason. At night she lay by his side listening to him breathe. She was not blind to his faults: his boyish egotism, his petty vanities, his tendency to mislead people. Nevertheless, he had cracked a door into her soul, where light and air now rushed in. For the first time in her life Medea did not feel alone.

On a bright afternoon in early autumn, the *Argo* entered the Saronic Gulf, and later the same day sailed into Piraeus, the busy port of Athens. For twenty-odd crewmen whose homes were in the south of Greece, this was the end of the voyage. To them, Jason distributed the last of his treasure. Many wept as they embraced their comrades, vowed to see each other again, exchanged tokens. At sunset Jason and Medea accompanied Phalerus, the only Athenian crewman, on the dusty road up to the city to meet his cousin, King Aegeus.

The gleaming marble temples whose melancholy ruins now crown Athens would not be built for another seven hundred years. Yet there were temples on the acropolis even then, simpler structures of stone and wood, dedicated to the same Olympian gods, and they stood alongside common shops, animal paddocks, granaries, public wells, and private dwellings. The most formidable structure was the palace.

Aegeus met the party in his own private quarters. A tall, gaunt figure, his white hair and lined face making him appear older than his fifty-five years, Aegeus was dressed simply and wore no crown. His eyes crinkled as he embraced Phalerus. Then he held the young man at arm's length to have a look at him. "You seem well. Did you get to use that famous bow of yours?"

"No, my lord. No battles, I'm afraid."

"Count that good fortune. Enough battles come your way uninvited."

Phalerus presented Jason.

"So you're the man who sought the Golden Fleece. Well, you fit the part. You're quite a dashing fellow. Did you get your prize?"

"I did, my lord, and it's quite a wonder. We have it under guard back at the ship if you'd like to see it."

"Thank you, no. I've seen enough wonders. I suspect it's caused you sufficient trouble already. Let it be." He turned to the third member of the party.

Jason introduced her. "This is the Princess Medea from Colchis."

"From Colchis?"

"She's the daughter of King Aeëtes," Jason added.

Aegeus peered into her crossed eyes. "You have left your homeland, Princess. Why?"

Jason drew breath to reply for her, but the king stopped him with a gently raised hand.

Medea said, "My lord, I married this gentleman."

"Did your father fashion the alliance?"

"No, my lord. He was not aware of it, nor would he have approved."

Aegeus frowned, lowered his eyes only for a moment. Then he offered Medea his arm. "You must be hungry, all of you. Dine with me tonight."

* * *

At the king's suggestion Phalerus escorted Jason through the acropolis after dinner while Aegeus invited Medea to tour the palace garden. The curved path was bathed in milky moonlight, the air scented with flowers.

"I love it back here," he said. "I hide out when I can't stand being a king anymore. Sometimes I think I would have preferred the life of a gardener."

"I had a garden in Colchis."

"Did you?"

Her attention was drawn to a clump of violet blossoms. She knelt and caressed the tapered petals pointing stiffly upward.

"They're curious, aren't they?" Aegeus commented. "Crocuses are supposed to come up in the spring, but these sprout every autumn without fail."

"At home we call them meadow saffron."

"Meadow saffron. What a lovely name!"

"Every part is poisonous."

"My God, are you certain?"

"A single leaf can kill you." She sniffed her fingertips, stood up again. "I made a specialty of poisons."

Aegeus laughed. "Splendid! Every family should have at least one expert poisoner. Keep the relatives honest!" He settled onto a bench nestled in a grape arbor and patted the space next to him. "Relatives!" he repeated. "They're worse than enemies sometimes, far worse. My grandfather, Cecrops, had to fight his three younger brothers to keep them from stealing the throne. Then his son, Pandion, had to fight *his* brother's sons for the same reason. Pandion was my father, and when he died, didn't I have to defend it against my younger brothers as well? It's never-ending, Medea."

"Jason always tells me how civilized Greece is."

"Wishful thinking, I'm afraid. None of us is very civilized when you come right down to it. The best we can hope for is a small improvement, a little advancement. Plow a new field so people eat better, make a law so things aren't quite so unfair. It's a frustrating business being a king. People think you can do whatever you want, but in fact you have damn little effect in the long run. Everything is compromises and partial solutions, half-measures and half-remedies."

Medea smiled. "Arf and arf."

"I beg your pardon."

"I'm sorry, my lord. You just reminded me of something that an old servant used to say. He was from the country and spoke with a peculiar accent. Whenever you'd ask him how things were going, he would say, 'arf and arf.' He meant half good and half bad."

"I like that. I'll have to remember it. That sums up a lot of life, doesn't it? Half good and half bad. If I ever have a son, I'm going to tell him that."

"You have no son, my lord?"

"Neither son nor daughter. My wife and I long for a child. To please my council, I even sent an embassy to Delphi. As usual, the oracle was inexplicable."

"May I know what she said?"

"Certainly. 'Don't unstop the wineskin until you reach the ancestral hearth.' Well, if the ancestral hearth is anywhere, it's here in the palace, since I was born here and so were my father and his father. But as for the rest, I'm at a loss. I've poured so much wine on the hearth that the stones are turning red."

Medea sat in thought. Then she said quietly, "Perhaps you and the queen are ... trying too hard."

"Oh?"

"Wait for a time, my lord—a week or two."

Mild surprise on his features, Aegeus flushed slightly when he understood what she was suggesting. "A week or two," he repeated. "Well, I suppose I can do that." He leaned back on the bench. "But now, Medea, tell me more about Colchis. King Aeëtes is your father?"

"Yes. He traces his line back to Helius, god of the sun."

"Indeed. And what's Aeëtes like? Is he a tyrant, wicked and cruel?"

"He's not cruel, my lord, but he does have a wicked temper."

"I like him already. Can he curse?"

"Like a field hand."

"Better and better! I always wanted to be able to curse with style, but I don't have the flair for it. He sounds like a capital fellow. I wish I could meet him."

"He wouldn't share that wish, my lord. He mistrusts Greeks."

"And yet, here you are among Greeks, married to one and determined to live the rest of your days with them." He paused. "I've cast aspersions on relatives, but sometimes family is all you have."

"Jason is my family now."

He knitted his brows. "It's not going to be easy for you, Medea, living in a foreign land. Tolerance is a rare commodity the world over. Here in Athens we have a sacred tradition of offering sanctuary to fugitives from other cities, even those who have committed heinous crimes. But foreigners? I've seen our citizens accept outright criminals more readily than they'd accept a law-abiding outlander." He heaved thoughtfully. "Of course, I'm probably being overly pessimistic, an annoying habit one acquires along with gray hair and aching bones. I like you, Medea. I'm not sure why. Maybe because there's something honest in your face. Or maybe because you're a king's child far from home, and I'm a king who wishes he had a child." He turned to her fully. "In any case, I want you to know that I'm your friend if you should ever need me. And I'll pray that your ancestor Helius keep an eye on you, as the sun keeps an eye on all of us. Now let's continue our stroll, and you can tell me if there are any other poisons in my garden."

She touched his arm. "You're a good man, my lord."

He smiled. "Arf and arf."

XII
Homecoming

CEOS, THEN ANDROS loomed off the starboard bow, then the pointed headland of Cape Caphereus off the port. Jason ticked off the landmarks as he impatiently paced the deck. Medea threaded a string of dried figs for him, and he picked at them absently as he watched the endless coast of Euboea slide slowly by. Finally, several long days later, they rounded Artemesium Point and entered his home waters, the Pagasaean Gulf. Jason half-expected a flotilla waiting to welcome him home, but only a few small fishing boats plied the bay. Startled mariners looked up from their nets as the great ship neared.

The harbor of Iolcus lay at the far end of the gulf, and when the *Argo* was spotted from shore, a small crowd gathered. As Jason's crew beached the ship, voices shouted out to him.

"Did you get to Colchis?"

"Did you pass through the Clashing Rocks?"

"Do you have the Golden Fleece?"

Jason just grinned and waved.

Richard Matturro

Two strong crewmen hefted the fleece, newly wrapped in a clean piece of sailcloth. Leading the way, Jason and Medea entered the city and threaded through the narrow streets toward the palace. There was triumph in his step now, for Jason no longer came as a supplicant. At the head of his small band of heroes, he came to demand his due.

Word of their arrival had preceded them, and soon Jason found himself in the center of the packed audience chamber. With satisfaction and pride he glanced around the hall at the expectant faces all turned toward him. It took a moment for him to notice the soldiers. They were arrayed discretely, behind the gawking nobles. A double row of the king's guards in full armor lined every wall. Suddenly uneasy, Jason looked over his shoulder at his diminished forces, outnumbered and surrounded.

King Pelias was not to be seen on the dais. Standing in his place was Acastus, Pelias's teenage son. Jason remembered Prince Acastus as a skinny, awkward, pimpled presence who had stood a step or two behind his father when Jason was last here. Blemishes still marred the young man's complexion, but now an oversized bronze crown sat crookedly upon his head.

"Well, Jason," Acastus trilled. "This is an unlooked-for pleasure."

"I ... I'm sorry, my lord," Jason said. "Where is King Pelias?"

"Dead, I'm afraid." Acastus lifted his chin slightly.

"Dead!"

"Alas, six weeks gone. The council," he nodded toward the group of solemn faces off to his right, "has ratified his decree that I succeed him."

Jason tried to conceal his dismay. "Forgive me, my lord. My condolences on your loss."

"He was full of years, and merciful Zeus took him in his sleep." Ceremoniously, Acastus now sat upon the throne. "But Jason, who is the charming lady at your side?"

"My lord, may I present the Princess Medea of Colchis."

Acastus raised an impertinent eyebrow. "Of Colchis! Well, your quest wasn't a total loss then."

"My quest, my lord, was a complete success." At his signal the two crewmen bore their burden forward and loosed the sailcloth, letting it fall to the floor.

An audible gasp went up from the onlookers, then murmuring as they jockeyed with each other to glimpse the wonder, but Acastus remained impassive. Wordlessly, and without undue hurry, he descended the platform and approached the fleece. Lightly he ran his fingertips over the gilded fur. "It's real," he said, more to himself than to anyone else.

"Quite real." There was pride in Jason's voice.

"Well, you never can tell. The Colchians might have made the whole thing up. You know how these outlanders are. No offence, Princess." Acastus flashed Medea a vapid smile. With a swirl of his robes, he turned and resumed his place upon the dais, then faced the company again. "You and your men are to be congratulated, Jason. At our leisure, you must tell the whole story of your adventure. But now, in honor of your return, I have taken the liberty of ordering a banquet for all of you. Please join me—"

"My lord," Jason interrupted, his voice controlled, determined. "King Pelias vowed in front of everyone in this hall that if I brought him the fleece, he would relinquish the crown to me in consideration of my father's rightful title."

Silence descended on the chamber. Acastus calmly folded his hands before him. "I am familiar with your father's claim, which, according to my best authorities, is inconclusive at best."

"*Inconclusive?*"

"As for Pelias, I am sorry to say that in his final years he began to lose that good judgment which we all so honored in him. You must understand that any capricious bargain he may have made with you was an outgrowth of his dotage, not state policy."

"*Wait a minute!* "

"Nevertheless, I feel a certain obligation toward you, Jason, and to your crew, since this misguided compact with my father doubtless cost you considerable time and fortune. So I am prepared to offer you a fair treasure in exchange for the Golden Fleece."

"You want to *buy* the fleece from me?!"

"Think of it as a reward. You are free, of course, to turn down my offer. But it occurs to me that what I give you might furnish handsome compensation to your men for their faithful service. Unless, of course, you have already so compensated them." There was a sly curl to his grin. "You needn't decide right away, Jason. For now, it is beholden upon all of us to celebrate your safe arrival and the success of your voyage. Let us eat and drink together."

With a final flourish, Acastus left the chamber. Too furious to move or even speak, Jason stared after him. He barely noticed Peleus draw near.

"What are you going to do?" Peleus hissed.

"Did you hear that little bastard? Reneging on a pact, a solemn pact his father made."

"I heard it, but there's not much we can do about it. There aren't even thirty of us left. We can't fight him. You're going to have to accept his offer."

"Like hell I am!"

Peleus took hold of his arm and pulled him closer, his voice urgent. "Listen, Jason, I know how you feel, but the men have worked hard for you, and they expect to take something home to show for it. If you try to send them off empty-handed while you still have the fleece—well, I needn't tell you the rest. Even if you got away with your life, you'd be vilified all over Greece. Take what the king offers. You have no choice."

In frustration Jason turned to Medea. "That crown is mine! It's mine by right."

Medea looked up at the platform, vacant now. Then she turned and fixed her eyes on Jason. Quietly she said, "It's a boy's crown."

"What are you saying?"

"Let the boy keep it. No one will even remember his name. But Jason will be known forever as the man who won the Golden Fleece."

* * *

Shining tripods, gold masks, silver urns, jeweled swords, six-layered shields with gods etched into the bronze: the treasure was copious. Jason had sold not only the fleece to Acastus, but his beloved *Argo* as well, since there would be no one left to man it. The fortune was conveyed down to the beach by cartload the next morning, and Jason distributed the entire lot to his expectant men, reserving for himself only a bit of gold and two riding horses. By late afternoon, Jason had said a sad final farewell to the last of his men, then stood on the beach alone with Medea. He gazed up at *Argo*'s proud figurehead.

"Hera abandoned me," he said.

"You don't know that, Jason."

He reached up and caressed the smooth, polished wood of the bow. "I think I'm going to miss this ship most of all." Jason sank down onto the sand and shook his head. "I can't believe it turned out like this. I don't know whether to laugh or cry. I built the greatest vessel afloat. I assembled the best men of my generation, took them to the end of the earth and back again, won the most famous prize in the world. And now, what did it all come to?"

She touched his shoulder. "Your life's not over."

"It might as well be. I never made any plans other than to live here and reign. Hell, I'm not fit for anything else." He lifted a fistful of sand and watched it run through his fingers. "What am I going to do? Where am I going to go?"

"We have the whole world, Jason."

"That's a joke."

"We have the whole world," she repeated more insistently, "and all the time in the world. We can do anything, go anywhere."

"Where would you suggest we go?"

She was silent for a moment. "Which way to Mount Pelion?"

"East," he said, pointing inland toward the ridge. "But I can't go there."

"Why not? It's where you came from."

"That's just the point. If I go back there, everyone will know I failed. Besides, I don't want to live in Mount Pelion anymore. I always wanted to get out of there."

"We're not going to stay. We'll just go for a visit."

He looked up at her. "But why?"

Medea turned to the mountain range in the distance. "I want to meet my mother-in-law."

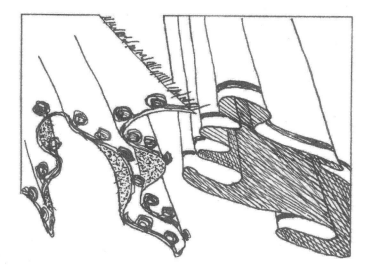

XIII
Relatives

POLYMELE ARCHED BACKWARD, pushing her fists into her aching lower spine, then glowered at the rows of cabbages as if they were so many ranks of mortal enemies. Even after two decades she still resented working the fields. What was a queen doing grubbing around in the dirt? Her earlier life in the aristocracy seemed a dream to her now. She had been a pretty young wife back then, and her husband Aeson a handsome prince. They had just sat down to dinner when the messenger burst into the room. Cretheus was dead.

Eagerly they had packed up their new baby and all their belongings and hurried toward Iolcus, but they were too late. The old king's bastard, Pelias, had seized the throne. Aeson was killed, but Polymele with her infant son escaped to neighboring Mount Pelion, where the locals, taking pity on the young mother and child, offered sanctuary and a share in their hardscrabble existence. Yet Polymele never abandoned her vision of royalty. Carefully she hid away the treasure she'd carried with her so that one day Jason could claim his birthright.

She squinted up at the sun. Two hours more before she could quit. Sighing, she dragged her sleeve across her forehead and was about to bend to her weeding again when she heard shouts from across the field.

"Polymele! Polymele!"

The bulky figure of her neighbor, Urana, was lumbering toward her. Out of breath when she finally came to a stop, she steadied herself by gripping Polymele's shoulder.

Urana panted, "I've run all the way from the village, and on a hot day like this! I'm like to drop dead right here. Lord Zeus lounging on Olympus! I must think I'm still sixteen. I used to run through these fields like an elk, like a lusty elk that courts in the woods! Lithe and blithe—that's what I was in those days—lithe and blithe, and look at me now!"

Polymele glared at the rough hand on her shoulder and barely restrained the urge to shake it off.

"I never grew up. That's what my Battus tells me. I'm still sixteen up here," she laughed, tapping her head with her finger. "Still think I can run through the fields like a lusty elk."

"Yes, well, what *did* you run here for?" Polymele asked irritably.

Urana faced her fully now. "What's the best news I could bring you?"

"Please, I don't have time—"

"It's your boy!"

Polymele's eyes opened wide. "What?"

"Your boy. He's come back!"

"Jason? Where?"

"At your house, waiting for you. And bless him, he looks as good as ever. Curly hair like Apollo, he has. And he's—"

But Polymele was no longer listening. Breaking free, she ran, walked, ran again toward home. Jason! It had been over a year since she'd seen him. Had he succeeded? Would this mean an end to hard labor? No more sore back, chapped hands, reddened skin. No more peasants hooting her name across the field. Could she finally return to the life she was born to?

As she approached her cottage, she spotted him leaning in the doorway. Polymele halted fifty feet away and looked at him. Jason seemed different somehow. What was it? Did he appear older? More serious? Or was it just an illusion, a result of the long absence? A tentative half-smile on his lips, he said quietly, "Hello, Mother."

Polymele spread her arms. Dutifully, he approached and embraced her. After examining his features up close, she asked, "How *are* you, Jason?"

"I'm fine."

"And did you reach Colchis?"

"Yes."

She hesitated. "Well?"

"If you mean the Golden Fleece, yes, I got it."

There was an unguarded flash of joy in her eyes, followed almost immediately by doubt. "But you're unattended, no servants, no retainers. Haven't you been to Iolcus yet?"

"Well, I'm going to explain all of that."

She took his arm. "Of course. Time enough later. You must be starved. Come on in."

"Mother, I want to introduce someone."

Polymele stopped short. "Oh, one of your men! I've heard they're from some of the best families in Greece."

"It's not one of the men, Mother."

At that moment a slender figure appeared in the doorway. Polymele's hand dropped from Jason's sleeve.

"Mother, this is the Princess Medea from Colchis—my wife."

* * *

Without comment Polymele listened to her son's whole story while she frowned at the rough wooden table between them. When he was finished, Jason said, "I'm sorry, Mother. I never imagined that Pelias might be dead. It was just rotten luck, I guess."

"Rotten luck," she repeated flatly.

"Either that or the gods never intended for me to be king."

Polymele sighed deeply, disgustedly. "And the fleece is gone too, and the ship, and the treasure, all gone." Her hand landed flatly on the table. She shook her head, making no attempt to hide her disappointment. When she looked up, she felt the unsettling crossed eyes of her new daughter-in-law staring at her. "But you have a wife."

"Yes, I do."

"That's good. No one should be alone. I just wish you had postponed the wedding until you got home. I would like to have ... attended."

"I didn't want to wait."

Polymele cast a mirthless grin at Medea. "My son is very impulsive, as you've probably learned. It's an endearing quality in youth and doubtless makes a young man seem charming, but it can lead into trouble too. Don't you agree, Medea?"

"In my country, we have a saying: sometimes it's better to jump out the window first, and then decide whether to fall."

"What a strange notion."

"It's only a proverb, Madam."

"Oh, no need to be so formal. I'm not a queen any longer— nor am I likely to become one again," she added, with a glance to her son. "You can call me Poly—"

"Mother," Jason broke in.

Both women looked at him.

"You can call her 'Mother,' " Jason clarified.

Icily Polymele concurred. "Yes, do call me 'Mother,' by all means."

"Thank you, Madam, but it is not considered proper in my country. Only the rustics take such liberties."

"How quaint! Well, you'll probably find we have quite a few rustic habits here, Medea. It comes of living so closely with the common people. I've warned Jason that if we're ever among quality again, we won't even know how to behave. You'll just have to get used to our provincial ways if you're going to stay here."

"We're not staying," Jason interjected. "We're just here to visit."

"What are you planning to do?"

He lifted his shoulders. "I don't know yet."

"Where are you planning to go?"

"I don't know that yet either." Jason paused, then exchanged a private smile with Medea. "We have the whole world."

Polymele's lips tightened. "I see."

* * *

He was aboard the *Argo* again, standing in the bow, feeling the stiff breeze on his face, the swell under his feet. Jason couldn't remember if he was on his way to Colchis or on his way home, but he was joyful, free, and full of expectation once more. Like fingers the wind lifted his hair, gently separated the locks, massaging his scalp. It was a pleasant feeling at first, but grew more insistent, more distracting, until it supplanted all other sensations in his dream. Instinctively Jason reached up, then woke with a start when he felt another hand stroking him. He blinked at the dim form of Polymele bending over him.

"Mother!" he hissed. "What are you doing?"

She put her finger on his lips and motioned for him to follow her. Careful not to wake Medea, who slept by his side, he wrapped a mantle about him. His mother was outside seated on the stone wall. Jason hoisted himself up next to her.

"A clear night," Polymele mused, gazing at the sky. "Can you make out the Great Bear?"

Jason followed her eyes upward to the crooked line of stars. "You didn't wake me up for stargazing."

"I just wanted a chance to talk with my son alone for a while. Is that so bad? You've been away a long time."

"What do you want, Mother?"

"Nothing."

"Listen, I know you well enough. What do you want?"

She smiled at him. "You're clever, clever enough to be a king."

"Well, I'm not going to be a king, so there's no use in talking about it anymore."

"Then let's talk about your future. Romantic notions notwithstanding, you don't really have the whole world, Jason. Most places won't be very hospitable."

"If you're trying to talk me into staying here, you may as well forget it."

"I'm not. There's nothing for you here. You should settle someplace where you have prospects of success, and I'd like to help you."

He eyed her. "How?"

"We have connections with ruling families in other cities. They may not have been anxious to take in a destitute mother and her baby twenty years ago, but now that you're grown and you've achieved a reputation for yourself, they might be willing to employ you."

"As what?"

"An official of some kind, an officer perhaps. You've had experience as a commander. The alternative, of course, is for you to do farm work like I do. Perhaps you would prefer manual labor. I hear there's dignity in it."

He turned away and was quiet for a few moments. "Tell me about these 'connections.' "

"Well, there's King Creon in Corinth for one. His great-grandfather was your father's uncle."

Jason snorted. "His great-grandfather was my father's uncle! Well, that's just dandy. And what exactly does that make me?"

"That, dear boy, makes you a relative. Let me tell you something about the world, Jason. People are much more likely to assist a stranger who's a relative than a stranger who isn't. Corinth is a peaceful, civilized, and prosperous city. Creon himself is a competent and fair-minded ruler, *and*—"

"And what?"

"He doesn't have a male heir."

"You never give up, do you?" Jason fell silent, chewing his lip. "How old is he—this Creon?"

"He's in his sixties, and a widower."

"He could marry again, someone younger, and still have a son."

"He could, but it's unlikely."

"He must have closer relatives than us in any case."

"Not living in Corinth, and not with such a reputation as you now have."

"Well, I'll think about it."

"Do. And while you're thinking, reflect on this too: you have a lot going for you, Jason, but you also have a major liability."

"What's that?"

"Your wife."

"What's wrong with Medea?" Jason snapped.

"Nothing's wrong with her, except that she's a foreigner. She looks different. She talks different. Wherever you go people will be wary of her—and of you too, by implication. If Creon has qualms about her, he might not risk giving you a position of authority."

"Then screw Creon!"

"The erudition of youth. Jason, don't you understand that I'm trying to help you?"

"I know exactly what you're doing. You don't like Medea, and you want me to turn my back on her."

Polymele assayed a weak protest.

"There's no use in denying it," Jason continued. "I know you don't approve of our marriage, but I don't care. Medea's my wife, and she stays with me. Besides," he added softly, "something happened back in Colchis. She made a big sacrifice for me."

"I see."

"Do you?"

"Certainly. I'm sure anyone who found himself in someone else's debt would propose marriage as the only suitable thanks."

Jason shot her a dark look.

"Well, my son, I just want you to be aware of the price you'll be paying. You've had an adventure now that will make you the talk of Greece. You'll be called a hero, like the great heroes of old. It's the stuff of legends. If you capitalize on that glory, Jason, you can snatch the golden future you were destined for. But if you spurn fortune and choose a mundane life—well, I just want you to know what you're giving up."

"I won't abandon her."

"A noble sentiment, Jason. I hope it's a comfort to you in your obscurity."

XIV
Hecate's Spell

JASON'S PEOPLE called it the Aegean. Shielding her eyes from the blazing sun, Medea peered at the hazy, flat, blue-gray horizon in the distance. Greeks had a name for everything. They even presumed to name the great water body that touched her own land—the "Black Sea." But to Medea it was all Ocean, the vast river that circled the world, and she felt an odd comfort knowing that waves rolling toward shore here might have glistened on the pebbled beach of Colchis mere days before. She leaned back against the gnarled old olive tree and closed her eyes. Was she homesick? No, not exactly that. But she missed her brother, her garden, the familiar rhythms that had made up her life.

A whinny interrupted her reverie. The chestnut mare, one of the two mounts they had ridden from Iolcus, was straining its tether toward grass just out of reach. Medea rose to her feet, and suddenly the world went black. Head spinning, she staggered into the tree, clutched it blindly, pressing her cheek against the rough bark. A full dizzying minute went by, and then as quickly as it had come, the fit was past. Medea looked around. The horse, the hilltop, the tranquil sea far below: everything was as it had been before.

Yet it was not. Directly her vision blurred again, this time from the tears that had inexplicably welled up in her eyes.

* * *

"You didn't eat anything!" Urana exclaimed, emptying the woolen pouch.

Medea collapsed into a chair. "I'm sorry. I wasn't hungry."

"I wish that would happen to me once in a while," Urana laughed. "Lord Zeus, I'm always hungry! That's why I look the way I do. You probably won't believe it, but when I was your age, I was as slim as you, Medea. Not quite as pretty, but pretty enough. Six different fellows wanted to marry me." She broke off and stuck her head out the door. "Menos? *Menos!* Are you watching your sister?"

Muffled words from outside.

"How you're supposed to be watching your sister while you're fighting off the whole Theban army, I'll never know."

More words.

"Yes, well, whatever army. See to it that you keep an eye on her, you hear me?" She returned to the table. "Boys! Battus carves him a wooden sword, and he thinks he's General Hercules! Now, where was I?"

"Six men wanted to marry you."

"That's right, six! And one of them was rich too. Well, sort of rich, but I chose a farmer instead. Same old story, heart over head. I bet you had a whole slew of suitors back where you came from."

"No, I never had any."

"Really? Shame on those fellows! Well, you've got a real handsome one in Jason, that's for sure, like one of the Immortals. Good looks run in that family. His mother was a beauty when she first came here. Every eligible bachelor in the district had his eye on her."

"But she didn't remarry?"

"No, never gave another man a bit of encouragement. She refused to marry beneath her, and she considered everyone in Mount Pelion beneath her. How are you getting on with her?"

"Not very well, I'm afraid."

Urana nodded knowingly. "Don't take it personal. She's a difficult one, Polymele is, more stubborn than a jackass walking backward. Luckily Jason's nothing like his mother. He gets along with everybody, doesn't look down his nose at anyone. He'll make you a fine husband." She paused, her face clouding over. "So tomorrow you leave."

"We're going to a place called Corinth. Jason says he's distantly related to the royal family there. I don't know if that will count for anything, but it might be a start for us."

"Well, I don't mind telling you that I'm going to miss you. I've grown fond of you over the past month, Medea. When I heard Jason married a princess, I expected you'd be stuck-up, but you're real down-to-earth. Don't take this the wrong way, but you don't act like a princess."

"That's exactly what my family used to say."

Urana bustled over to the fire and stirred the large bronze pot. "How about some nice barley with goat's milk?"

"I'd like that. Thank you."

She ladled the bubbling mixture into a wooden bowl and placed it on the table. Suddenly Medea felt ill.

"What's the matter?" Urana asked. "Something wrong with it?"

"No, it's just that—"

"Lord Zeus, you look green."

Medea pushed the bowl away. "I don't know what's wrong. Up at the top of Mount Pelion this morning I nearly fainted."

Urana's brow furrowed. "If you don't mind me asking, has your 'session' been regular?"

"My session?"

"I don't know what you call it in your country. You know, your monthly—"

Medea's crossed eyes focused inward. "We call it 'Hecate's

spell.' "

"Hecate's spell? That's a new one on me. Who's Hecate?"

"She's ... a goddess that I'd almost forgotten."

"Never heard of her. Well, has your 'spell' been on schedule?"

"No."

"How many have you missed?"

"Two."

Urana's face lit up. "Well then, you may miss several more. In fact your Madame Hecate may not visit you for some time!" She bounced from her chair now and threw her arms around Medea. "Oh, my dear! Congratulations! It looks like you're starting a family. Lord High Zeus, now I'm really sorry you're leaving. I'd love to be there when your time comes. I do love babies, and I know yours is going to be beautiful, good looking couple like you and Jason." She squeezed Medea, then pulled her own chair closer. "Don't you worry about the sickness. It'll pass. And you have to eat, sick or not, because you'll be eating for two now. So why don't you give that barley another try."

Medea stared at the steaming bowl. "When do you think—?"

"Well, let's see. Two months gone, that means it'll be sometime in the spring."

"I never expected to have children. I never thought I wanted them."

"It'll change when your little one comes. You'll be surprised. You'll find love in you that you never knew was there. Also patience, and endurance—and a strong stomach," she laughed.

But Medea was trembling. "I'm scared."

Urana took her hand and patted it. "Don't worry. Fear is like a stone lion: terrible to look at, but when you get up close, you find out the fangs are dull and harmless."

* * *

Jason was bending over the drainage ditch raking the shovel along the channel to clear away debris, a job he must have done a hundred times while he was growing up here. Medea felt a curious pleasure as she watched him work with his hands. When he straightened up, he spotted her and waved. She tied the mare behind the cottage and joined him.

"I'm trying to get a few last things done for Mother before we leave," he explained.

"Can I help?"

"I'm nearly finished," he shrugged.

Together they squatted over the furrow and began removing the accumulated rocks and leaves. After a few moments as Medea pulled a tangled vine free, she said calmly, "I'm pregnant."

For an instant Jason's expression went blank. The next thing Medea knew, she was being hoisted in his arms and spun around. Astonishment vied with joy in his features. "Are you sure?"

"Yes, pretty sure."

"I can't believe it," he said, hugging her. "When I thought about this before, I imagined … oh, I don't know what I imagined. Having some little heir to the throne, I guess, and starting a dynasty, not a family. But this child won't be a prince. It will just be our son—or our daughter—and you know what? I don't care." He pulled back and looked at her again, his face serious now, his voice earnest. "Everything I've wanted in life, Medea, was in someone else's hands, either to withhold from me or take away from me. But this child will be ours! Do you know what I'm saying? No one, *no one*, can take it away." He embraced her again and whispered in her ear, "I love you, Medea."

And Medea clung to him. The portal, sought, fled from, ignored, always elusive, finally stood open before her. She whispered back, "I love *you*, Jason."

That evening when she was alone preparing for bed, Medea removed the ever-present dagger from her belt, looked at it for a long moment, then carefully wrapped it in a cloth and put it away in the leather bag she had carried all the way from Colchis.

XV
Corinth

THERE WERE NO INNS in those days, no cheerful taverns with roaring fires where a weary traveler could expect a hot meal and a comfortable bed. To find better shelter than an overhanging bough during the two-week journey to Corinth, Jason and Medea had to depend on the hospitality of strangers along the way. Such kindness was not uncommon. Receiving wayfarers was a pious obligation sanctioned by Zeus himself, and so the couple were often welcomed in cottage and farmhouse. When they were not, they slept under a tree.

The autumn rains came early and turned the dusty roads into sloughs of mud, slowing their progress to a crawl. Medea was sick most mornings, and the constant jostling on her horse did nothing to ease things. Worst of all, though, was what was happening to her body, which seemed less and less her own. As the being grew inside her, nurturing itself on her blood, it made her blanch or blush, ache or tire, all without her assent. In the long hours of silence as she plodded along the rutted paths with Jason, she repeated to herself the outlandish words she had spoken so matter-of-factly: "I'm pregnant." How could such a world of dreadful import be hidden in so small a phrase?

They rode through the pastures of Thessaly, forded the broad River Sperchius, trod within sight of Mount Parnassus, where the Muses dwelled. Still heading southward, they passed the olive groves and vineyards of Boeotia, then finally, on the thirteenth day, rounded the Gulf of Corinth and turned west. A heavy rain greeted them on the morning Jason and Medea crossed the isthmus from mainland Greece to the broad plains of the Peloponnese. At the end of the narrow land bridge they pulled their horses to a halt. Looming in the distance, shrouded in drizzle and fog, was the indistinct outline of a great double peak.

"That must be it," Jason said, his voice unusually hushed.

"How far away?"

"A few more miles. Do you need to rest?"

"No, I'm all right."

They gazed at the ghostly form thrusting up from the plain, but neither made a move to go.

* * *

In earliest times the city of Corinth had been called Ephyra, and during the long ages before memory Ephyra doubtless had its own eventful history, a thousand tales of madness, death, war, treachery, and revenge, all lost to us now. Only the name survives, mentioned occasionally as a dim recollection. Corinth was the new city built upon the old, and intended, as all new cities are, to bury the past, as if ancient horrors can be broken up as rubble to line the cellar. Mocking such naïve intentions, fate saw to it that one of Corinth's very first citizens was Sisyphus, condemned for eternity to roll a great stone up a hill in the underworld only to see it tumble back to the bottom again. His crime? The ultimate reformer, Sisyphus had shackled Death, our common, oldest enemy. But the gods, wiser and more careful, loosed the fetters, and they devised for Sisyphus a punishment that at once caricatures the human condition and teaches the value of death, which sets us free of it.

The rain still falling incessantly upon them, Jason and Medea slowly approached the city gates of Corinth. When they had dismounted and passed through, they found themselves in a large market square, bustling with people despite the downpour. A boy tottered by with a squirming lamb draped over his shoulders.

Jason hailed him. "Excuse me. Which way to the palace?"

The boy eyed the bedraggled strangers, then motioned with his head toward the peaks that stood it the very center of the city. "Up there."

Barely discernible on the higher of the two promontories was a rocky parapet.

"Take the royal road." The boy pointed with his nose toward the far end of the marketplace. "Quarter-mile, straight up."

As the boy scurried off with his burden, Jason watched his bare feet splash through the puddles on the wide stone plaza. "It's paved!" Jason exclaimed. "The whole square is paved!"

Already fatigued, Medea would have preferred not to make the climb to the upper city today, but she followed Jason along the steep, winding track. An hour later, exhausted, they staggered through a second pair of massive bronze gates. Perched on a mountaintop, and separated from the road by a sheer rock cliff and stone battlements, the citadel was buzzing with activity. Workmen with baskets of bricks strapped to their backs elbowed with goats being herded through alleyways. Past the shops and stables and private homes, Jason and Medea finally came to the palace on a raised outcrop all by itself.

Jason ran his fingers through his dripping hair and with as much dignity as he could muster identified himself to the guards at the entry. His name instantly recognized, the couple was escorted through a courtyard where their horses were led away by palace grooms. Under the shelter of a portico, a servant ushered them into the king's chambers where Creon was awaiting them.

"Jason, welcome!" he boomed, grasping the younger man's hand firmly with both his own. Creon was a thickset man in his middle sixties, bald except for a fringe of gray. His dress was simple but rich, and his crown a jewel-studded gold band. He seemed a man comfortable in his role as king, used to power, but, after a lifetime in the public eye, no longer mindful of the difference between the authentic and the useful. "I've heard about your exploits. You're quite famous here. I wish I'd had a young kinsman to represent Corinth in your crew."

"I would have liked that, Sir." Jason presented his wife. "May I introduce the Princess Medea of Colchis."

"Welcome, my dear. And how do you find our country?"

"Wet, my lord."

His laugh was hearty. "So it is. And in summer, hot as hell and dry as dust. You'll see." He turned back to Jason now and assumed a more sober demeanor. "Your mother's message informed me about that bad business back in Iolcus. I never met your father, Jason, but I did meet your grandfather once, King Cretheus. He was a good man, a very good man. Your father should have succeeded him, and you your father, but, alas, these things are in the hands of the gods. In any case, I'll see to it that Iolcus's loss will be Corinth's gain. I can use a resourceful young man."

"Thank you, Sir."

"I hope to thank *you*," he countered, squeezing Jason's shoulder to emphasize the point, "but for now, it's time both of you got some dry clothes and some rest. I've arranged rooms for you quite close to the palace, which I trust you'll find suitable. Take a few days to settle in. Walk around the city; get to know it. Then, when you're ready to go to work, come back. I have plenty for you to do."

* * *

Gently the servant closed the door behind her, leaving them alone in their new lodgings. The rooms were spacious, lavishly furnished, and despite the weather outdoors, bright and airy. New clothing had been laid for them on the bed, and on a polished table sat an ornate amphora of wine and a platter piled high with olives, cheese, bread, and fruit.

"Are you hungry," Jason asked as he plucked several grapes

and popped them into his mouth.

Medea sat on the edge of the bed watching him. She said, "Your mother."

"What about her?"

"She contacted Creon. Coming here was her idea, wasn't it?"

"She suggested it. That's all."

"Why didn't you tell me?"

He breathed deeply. "I was afraid if you knew Mother had anything to do with it, you would have refused to come."

Medea lifted one of the gowns. The immaculate white chiton was smooth, finely woven. "I don't need any of this, Jason."

"Maybe you don't, Medea, but you're going to have a baby. I don't want our child born in a ditch. If Corinth turns out to be a good place for us, what does it matter if it was Mother's idea?"

A sudden spasm made Medea grimace.

"Are you all right?" Jason went to her and knelt at her feet, resting his cheek on her belly. "Listen, I'm sorry I didn't tell you, Medea." His eyes swept the room. "You're right, we don't need any of this, but I do need my self-respect. Try to understand: everything I've done so far has been a failure, but now I have a second chance. I'm going to have a family, and I want my family to be proud of me."

"I'm proud of you already."

Jason looked up at her. "If you want to leave, Medea, we'll leave tomorrow."

She was quiet for a moment while she stroked his curly hair. "No. Let's eat."

XVI
Servants of Aphrodite

CREON ASSIGNED JASON a number of small tasks that seemed arbitrary and undemanding. One day he took an inventory of weapons in the armory. Another day he measured the water level in four city wells. Still another day he walked the western rampart, looking for breaches in the wall. Nevertheless, Jason was glad to be employed and threw himself conscientiously into the work, doing more than was required.

While her husband was thus engaged, Medea spent the days acquainting herself with her new home. Corinth was a labyrinthine tangle of narrow, unmarked streets and alleys, baffling to a newcomer, and Medea regularly lost her way. Turning a corner on one occasion she found herself at the foot of a great stone temple that occupied the highest point in the upper city. She mounted the steps and passed into the dimly-lit interior. A chorus of giggles ceased with the sound of her footfalls, and a young woman appeared. Sixteen or seventeen years of age, she was dressed in a nearly transparent, flowing gown. She lowered her eyes shyly.

"Madam, how may I help you?"

"I just came to visit," Medea explained.

The young woman seemed puzzled.

"I thought I would pay my respects," Medea added, "to the god—or goddess—here."

Two other women emerged from the shadows. They too wore revealing gowns, but were closer to Medea's own age. The elder of the two stepped forward. "Welcome to the Temple of Aphrodite, Princess Medea."

"You know my name."

"Forgive me, Madam. We heard of your arrival with Jason. We don't see too many unfamiliar faces. I am Lyctaea. This is Nereis," she said, indicating the young woman, "and this is Theope."

"Are you priestesses?"

Lyctaea made a small curtsy. "We are the Servants of Aphrodite."

"The temple harlots," Theope clarified.

Lyctaea's eyes rolled. "You must forgive Theope, Madam. She has an abrupt manner, but means no disrespect. We do indeed serve the men of Corinth, and within these confines that service is considered holy."

Medea was embarrassed. "I see. I'm sorry."

"Think nothing of it." Lyctaea's eyes strayed to the bulge beneath Medea's chiton. "When is your child due, Madam?"

"In the spring."

"I have two myself," Lyctaea announced proudly, "a boy and a girl."

There were footsteps again. A short, heavy-set man stood hesitantly in the entry. "Excuse me," he mumbled. "Is Nereis free?"

Lyctaea whispered to her young companion, "It's only Zagreus. He won't take long."

Zagreus placed an offering on the table in the vestibule, but all the while his attention was focused on Medea. "Are you new here?" he asked.

A note of warning in her voice, Lyctaea said sharply, "This is the Princess Medea, the *wife of Jason*."

"Oh, I'm sorry, Madam, so sorry." Bowing and scraping, Zagreus hurriedly retreated, Nereis in tow.

Lyctaea shook her head. "I apologize, Madam. Some of them have no sense at all. You see, we have very few female callers, just an occasional wife looking for her husband."

"It's all right."

"If you're not in a hurry, Madam, would you honor us in a libation to commemorate your visit?"

* * *

The temple interior was ringed with small, curtained chambers, the largest of which was used by the women as a common room. Lyctaea offered her guest a cushion, then poured out three cups of wine. Her eyes squeezed shut she intoned, "Lady Aphrodite, all praises of Corinth fly up to you, all blessings rain down upon us. Please bring good fortune to Princess Medea, long life and happiness." She opened her eyes and spilled the customary drop. Then she settled back again, and they all drank. "I hear that you're from the other side of the world, Madam."

"Colchis is very far away," Medea agreed. "And you, you're from another country too?"

Lyctaea shook her head. "We're Corinthians. You thought, perhaps, we were captives of war. No. At a very early age our lives were dedicated to the goddess." She lowered her voice. "Girl babies are not always wanted in Corinth. Among poor families, infant daughters are often exposed on the hillside. We are the lucky ones."

"Speak for yourself," Theope muttered. She had been staring at Medea's face. Now she inquired, "What's wrong with your eyes?"

"*Theope!*" Lyctaea snapped.

Medea turned to the other. "They've always been like this."

"They're kind of queer," Theope noted, leaning closer, "but not bad really. Does your husband like them? Sometimes men like odd things. Once I painted a little red spot right on my—"

Richard Matturro

"I'm sure the princess isn't interested," Lyctaea broke in firmly.

There were more footsteps. Lyctaea scrambled to her feet and disappeared. A few moments later she stuck her head through the curtain. "It's Sicyon."

"You or me?" Theope asked.

"He wants Nereis, but he'll settle for you."

Theope took a last gulp of wine, patted her lips, and slipped from the room.

"Nereis is new," Lyctaea explained, settling down again across from Medea, "so she's very popular right now. It was the same with me when I started, and Theope too. By the way, I hope you didn't take offense at the things she said. Theope's a kindhearted soul, really, but she lost a baby this past year—stillborn."

"Oh, I'm sorry."

"Yes, it was very sad. She wanted the child a great deal, and she hasn't been quite the same since. Theope's always been a little crazy, saying the wrong thing at the wrong time, but it's gotten much worse. We're praying no one complains to the priest. If she's expelled from the temple, I don't know what she'll do."

"How did this all come about?"

"You mean the Servants of Aphrodite?" Lyctaea shrugged. "I don't know. It's always been like this. Don't you have anything similar in your country?"

"We do, but it's not in a temple, and it's not considered—holy."

Lyctaea's lips formed into a wry smile. "Corinthians believe that every time we please a citizen, Aphrodite blesses the city."

"Do you believe that?"

"I believe … it's disagreeable to be exposed on the hillside."

* * *

Creon jutted his finger out the window. "That's the problem, right there."

Jason leaned out. The palace commanded a sweeping view of the isthmus several miles away. The Gulf of Corinth lay to the north, the Saronic Sea to the south, separated by a narrow strip of land.

"We're on the gulf side," Creon continued, "and it's an eight-day voyage all the way around the Peloponnese to get to open water. Every year ships founder making that trip."

He flopped disgustedly into a chair, but Jason continued to peer out the window. "What's on the ocean side, Sir?"

"Nothing. A nice harbor, but nothing else."

"It's so close."

"By land it's close. That's what's so damn frustrating, but it's not practical to carry goods overland. Anyway, Jason, you're an experienced navigator. I'm going to give you my ship, the royal barge, so you can go out and have a look. The master is my foreman, Evanus, who was in charge of that paving job you're so fond of, down in the market square. Take the ship, scout around a little, and see if you can find a safer route."

At that moment the door swung open. "Father, did you know that—. Oh, I'm sorry. I didn't realize you were busy."

"No, no, come in, Glauce," Creon said, rising and waving her forward. "You haven't met Jason yet. Jason, this is my daughter, Glauce."

Her auburn hair was swept on top of her head and held in place with jeweled pins. Her features were even, delicate. She thrust out her hand. "So this is the hero of the Golden Fleece. Father has told me a lot about you."

"Exaggerated, I'm sure, Princess."

"Of course," Creon quipped. "What's the point of having adventures if you can't exaggerate them? But Jason's most important achievement, as far as I'm concerned, will be finding us a better shipping route. That's the Golden Fleece I'm after."

"You'll have to forgive my father, Jason. He must carefully guard the secret that he has a romantic soul. Beneath that businesslike exterior beats the heart of a swashbuckler."

Creon threw back his head in a booming laugh.

"Because he spends his time on mundane matters of state," Glauce continued, "he doesn't consider himself a hero. But I've told him that digging culverts and dredging harbors are as much acts of heroism as slaying a gorgon."

"You see what I'm up against here," Creon added, winking at Jason.

"If the person closest to you does not see the hero, who will? Jason, surely your wife finds you heroic."

Jason smiled. "More than I deserve, I'm afraid."

"Nonsense. I don't believe that for a minute. But now that we've been properly introduced, you will stay for dinner with us."

"Do, Jason," Creon chimed in.

"Thank you, Sir. Thank you both, but I really can't. I have a dozen things I'm supposed to do."

"You see what comes of this, Father," Glauce scolded. "You get a good man, and you work him to death."

"Put them by, Jason," Creon told him. "Enough work for one day. Join us. And you can give Glauce a first-hand account of your adventures—with appropriate exaggeration!"

"Indeed," Glauce added, taking Jason's arm, "and first off you can settle a rumor I've heard. Did you really meet Hercules?"

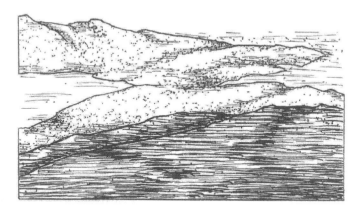

XVII
Screw Route

Evanus watched him from the stern. After a week he was still trying to size up his commander, this young newcomer. He passed the rudder to a companion, then picked his way forward. "We're coming up on the bone-yard now, Sir."

For his part, Jason too had been taking the measure of Creon's foreman. He looked at Evanus now, a wiry man of indeterminate middle age, his skin deeply lined and brown from the sun. "Bone-yard?" Jason repeated.

"That's what we call it. Bones of ships laid to rest there."

"What's the headland up on the left?"

"Taenarus Point." He gave his commander a sidelong glance. "The little one beyond it is Malea Point. They stick out the bottom of the Peloponnese like two teats on a cow's udder."

"And on the right?"

"That's Cythera, five miles offshore."

Jason gazed at the island in the distance. "The birthplace of Aphrodite, so they say, isn't it? Born of the sea-foam."

"Well, in our version, Sir, that particular 'sea-foam' was what bubbled out of Uranus's pecker after Chronos chopped it off and threw it in the ocean."

"Ouch," Jason winced.

"Didn't know that charming little tale, did you, Sir? Well, anyway, you've got two choices coming up, both bad. You can go between the island and the coast, which is shorter, but that's also where all the frigging rocks are, and the current's a bitch."

"And if you go around?"

"You go around, you add three to ten hours, depending on the weather. And there are ledges and reefs if you stick too close to the island."

"Can't you just give it a wide berth?"

"Sure you can, and add more hours. But wide or narrow, wind blows like a bastard on the ocean side." He flashed an ironic grin. "Aphrodite sure as hell doesn't make it easy for you to sail around her. We call the outside passage the love route—after her—and the inside passage the screw route—also after her. So, Sir, which will it be?"

"What do most sailors do?"

"Screw."

Jason snorted. "All right, then we'll screw too. We'll give love a try on the way back."

Evanus was a skilled pilot and had negotiated the tricky passage many times, but as he maneuvered the ship safely through the strait, Jason glimpsed vessels not so lucky, hulls shattered on the rocks, bare ribs poking up through the pounding waves. He heaved a sigh of relief when they passed into the open water again.

Another full day went by before they entered the Saronic Sea and sighted the southern edge of the isthmus. As evening approached, Evanus drew once more to Jason's side. "We'll need to stop for the night, Sir. If we go up the coast a little farther, we can dock at Crommyon. Not much of a town to look at, but they've got a certain house that—"

"Beach the ship here."

"Here?" Evanus viewed the barren coastline. "But there's nothing here."

"I know, but it's the narrowest part of the isthmus. I want to have a look around tomorrow."

When Evanus awoke the next morning, Jason was nowhere to be seen. Leaving the crew to prepare for departure, he hiked along the shoreline until he found his commander up on the plateau perched on a boulder. Peering inland, Jason was tapping a stick impatiently on the rock.

"Excuse me, Sir," Evanus said as he approached him. "We're ready when you are."

"Evanus, how far is it across?"

"Across the isthmus? Four miles, tops."

"So it took us eight days sailing all the way around the Peloponnese just to get to a point that's only four miles from where we started."

"That's one way of looking at it, but every city on the gulf has to do the same thing."

"It's absurd!" Jason rapped the stick so hard that it snapped in two. He threw down the slivered fragment to join the other. "Four miles! And not even hilly country. I know because I crossed it lengthwise when I first came to Corinth." He scowled and leapt down. "There's got to be a better way."

Noncommittal, Evanus folded his arms and rested his chin on his chest while Jason paced. "Wind's in our favor, Sir," he offered.

Jason came to a stop and glared at him, though he did not seem to be looking at Evanus at all. After a long silence he said simply, "You go without me."

"Sir?"

"Take the ship back to Corinth. I'll walk."

"Across the isthmus?"

"Why not? I'll be home by dinner."

As Jason marched off, Evanus ran his hand over the stubble on his chin. He called out, "What about the love route?"

To no one in particular Jason shouted, "Screw the love route!"

Medea was with her servant, Euterpe, sorting clothes. A spinster twenty years her senior, Euterpe had a somber disposition and was not given to chatter. Nevertheless, Medea was grateful for her company. Though people accorded Medea respect as the wife of Jason, they still viewed her as an outsider and kept their distance. Only Lyctaea, the Servant of Aphrodite, who was likewise shunned by most Corinthians, befriended her, and the irony of their connection was not lost on Medea. Now, with Jason away for the first time, Medea had no one to talk to. She held up a white chiton, the garment that had been laid out on the bed for her when they first arrived in Corinth.

"Isn't it clean, Madam?" Euterpe asked.

"No, it's fine," Medea assured her, folding it and putting it away.

Suddenly there was the loud clatter of footsteps hastily mounting the stairs, and the next moment Jason burst into the room. Out of breath, his face windburned, his cloak dusty, he caught Medea in his arms.

"I thought I wouldn't see you for another week," she said, hugging him.

"I took a shortcut." He squeezed Medea, kissed her hard on the lips, then glanced down at his soiled tunic doubtfully. "I've got to wash and change, go see the king. Euterpe, a bath, and hurry!"

"Why?" Medea asked as he let her go. "What happened?"

There was devilish glee in his eyes. "I found the answer to his problem."

* * *

"Portage!" Creon exclaimed.

"Yes."

"Across the isthmus."

"Yes."

Creon shook his head. "No, Jason, it's not feasible."

"Sir, it's only four miles. I walked it today in less than two hours."

"You weren't pulling a boat behind you."

"Yesterday I watched twenty men pull the royal barge completely out of the water and drag it up on the beach, something they do all the time."

"That's a far cry from hauling a loaded vessel out of the gulf, lugging it overland, and then depositing it back in the water on the ocean side. It's imaginative, Jason, but not reasonable."

"No offence, Sir, but a hazardous four-hundred-mile voyage around the Peloponnese is neither imaginative nor reasonable."

Creon was quiet for a moment. "You saw what the road was like."

"Of course," he shrugged. "It's bad: rocky, rutted, overgrown."

"You can't drag a ship, even of moderate size, over a road like that. You'd tear the ship—and the road—to pieces. And in the rainy season—."

"Sir, I wasn't suggesting using that road the way it is. We have to build a new one ... a paved road."

"*Paved!*"

"Yes, a paved road with rollers—logs, for the ships to roll on. Only a paved road would serve for portage that distance. It would be easier to maintain, and you could use it year-round, rain or shine."

Creon narrowed his eyes. "I don't think you realize the magnitude of the project you're suggesting. A paved road across the isthmus, wide enough for ships, would be a massive undertaking. Corinth isn't a city of slaves, you know. Where would the men come from who would build this road? I'll tell you. They would have to be Corinthian citizens who took time away from their farms, their shops, their families, and I'd have to make it worth their while to do so. How could we justify that expense, even if it saved us the trip around the Peloponnese?"

"That's the point, Sir. It wouldn't be just for us. There are a dozen cities on the gulf, every one of them in the same predicament we are, but we control the isthmus. If we build a portage road from Lechaeum to the Saronic Sea, those cities would pay us to use it.

Corinth would become the market port for the whole interior of Greece."

The king fell silent. He rose from his chair and stepped to the window from which he could see the two water bodies in the distance, their bulging shores so tantalizingly close to each other, and only the narrow land bridge between. He stood deep in thought for several minutes, then, almost to himself, said, "We'd need horses."

"Yes, Sir, teams of them at both ends to tow the ships."

"And if we have horses, then we'd need men to take care of them."

"And bunks for the men, and stables, and kitchens. And we'd need wagons, spare parts, tools. We'd need barns for storage."

"And a garrison."

"Yes, Sir, and a garrison." He paused. "Give me a hundred men, and I'll build that road in a year."

Slowly Creon turned around and eyed Jason. His tone was stern, threatening. "This is no youthful lark, Jason, like the Golden Fleece. What you're proposing here is a serious enterprise. If you do this—if I *allow* you to do this—much of Corinth's wealth and energy will be invested in it. Therefore, it had better be well thought out, well planned, and well executed, because there will be no walking away from it. Am I making myself very, very clear?"

Jason's eyes locked with his. "Yes, Sir."

"Good, because I want there to be no mistake about it." Creon turned back to the window. "Now leave me. I'll talk over your proposal with my council."

XVIII
Unexpected Visitors

SHE'D HAD A BOYISH, athletic frame. Running, riding, stretching herself to the limit had always held a secret joy for Medea. Now she grieved as if a trusted friend had deserted her. Distorted and weighed down by the creature growing inside, her body rebelled. Her breasts were sore and swollen; her teeth ached; pins prickled her feet. Yet these annoyances paled next to the distress in her soul. Regularly and for no apparent reason she would find herself weeping, wishing she were dead. And at a time when she needed him most, Jason was inaccessible.

The king had approved his plan to build a road across the isthmus, and Jason was put in charge of the whole enterprise. At first Medea was pleased at her husband's newfound fervor. He was up before dawn most mornings, eager to get going. Huddled with Evanus, his foreman, he was learning about surveying, grading, stone-cutting. He was also learning how to manage the men assigned to him, how to gain their respect, how to make his interest their profit. When he returned home in the evening, his face and hands caked with dust, his voice hoarse, he was happier than Medea had ever seen him. He would eat ravenously and tell her all about the day's progress, snags they'd encountered, solutions they'd worked out. Then, shortly after dinner, weariness would overtake him, and he'd go straight to bed.

Nights often found Medea wakeful, and when she did sleep, she was visited by bizarre nightmares. Once she dreamt that she had strayed to the work site. Unaware of her presence, Jason stood upon a mound shouting orders. She admired the self-confidence in his demeanor, the sense of purpose so long absent. Then to her horror Medea realized she was lying in the roadbed, and before she could escape, a huge block of stone fell on her chest knocking the wind out of her. She woke with a start, gasping for air. In the darkness she could hear the night bird's song and Jason's even breathing as he slumbered peacefully by her side.

Winter was a dreary, rainy, chill season in Corinth, but activity at the isthmus continued uninterrupted. Jason bragged once to Medea that his men, working at peak efficiency, could lay seventy feet of pavement a day. He said this with more pride than anything he'd ever told her before. Yet Jason was talking with her less about the project, less about everything. Some nights he would come home so exhausted he would hardly speak at all, and had to be coaxed to eat dinner before collapsing into bed. Their lovemaking became rare.

And as the winter dragged interminably, Medea's belly swelled larger and larger. No longer able to ride her horse, or to walk any great distance, she found just going about her day-to-day chores draining. She had trouble breathing most of the time, was tired all the time, yet sleep eluded her. It was a strain to stand, sitting was difficult, lying down near impossible. The furtive thing within had succeeded in dominating her whole life. Then, on a bright morning when the first wildflowers bloomed in the meadow, the pains began.

* * *

Euterpe had been drawing water. Upon her return to the

house, she was greeted by a muffled cry. Bathed in sweat, Medea was sitting on the edge of the bed, her face twisted in anguish. Tenderly Euterpe touched her shoulder. "Please, Madam, we've waited long enough. I'll fetch the midwife."

Presently a stout, imperious matron of sixty swept through the door trailing a younger companion. She cocked an eye at Medea, who lay panting on the bed. "How frequent?" she demanded of Euterpe.

"Very close, Ma'am. She's … quite frightened."

"Why didn't you call me sooner?"

"She didn't want me to. In her country—"

"Never mind what they do in her country," the grandam sniffed. "Fetch a blanket, some cloth, and fill a basin."

"Yes, Ma'am."

She strode to the foot of the bed and looked over her nose at Medea. "Now there's nothing to be afraid of, my dear. We've all been through this, and you'll get through it too. Iole's just going to shift you down a little and get you ready."

Medea had been following their movements with increasing alarm, her eyes bloodshot and hollow. As Iole reached toward her, Medea screeched wildly and lashed out with her nails, raking four ragged red lines into the woman's arm. Iole fell back in shock.

"Now listen here, Madam," the grandam warned, "we're trying to help you." She gestured for Iole to approach again, but Medea tensed, a threatening growl deep in her throat. "You see?" the grandam hissed to Euterpe. "This is what comes of marrying barbarians. Princess indeed! She's little better than a wolf that devours its own young. Get some cord."

"But—"

"Two pieces. Get it."

Armed with the lengths of rope, they stood on either side of Medea. The grandam nodded significantly to Iole. "Both at the same time. Ready?"

While she howled and thrashed, they pinioned Medea's arms and secured her wrists to the bedstead. Once subdued she went limp, a lull in her pains. Lifting her chiton, they drew up her

Richard Matturro

knees, and the grandam peered into the dark cavity. "It's in correct position," she assessed coolly.

A fresh pang hit her, and Medea's eyes popped open.

"All right, young lady, now push," the grandam commanded.

Medea spat out a string of appalling oaths that made Iole blanch. The grandam merely set her jaw and bent to work. "Push, my princess. Say whatever you'd like as long as you push. The quicker you help us, the quicker this will be over."

But it was not quick. Euterpe wrung her hands helplessly for twenty, forty, eighty minutes as she watched her mistress's agony. Finally, after a last pitiful cry that broke Euterpe's heart, it was done. While the grandam cut the umbilicus and tied it off, Medea lay spent upon the bed, gulping air. Iole wrapped the squirming, purple infant in a blanket.

"All this fuss for such a little fellow," the grandam commented, taking the child into her arms and examining it carefully. "You've had a fine little boy, Madam. You've borne Jason a son. You should be very proud."

Medea only trembled and closed her eyes. Euterpe ventured, "Is she all right?"

"Of course she's all right," the grandam assured her. "She'll be up and about in no time. Now here," she said, passing the child into Euterpe's hands, "take him away and bathe him."

Iole looked worried. "I think she's still in pain."

"Nonsense."

All three gathered around the bed now where Medea continued to quake and whimper uncontrollably.

"Can't you do something?" Euterpe pleaded.

"There is nothing to do!" the grandam snapped. "It was a perfectly good delivery."

The room grew strangely quiet. A minute passed. Two. Three. Then all at once the silence was shattered by the door flying open. "*Where is she?*" a deep-throated voice demanded.

Filling the entry was a tall figure in a flowing maroon cloak. She had fierce dark eyes with heavy bags slung under them, her mouth drawn into a permanent frown, her long black hair streaked with gray. She spotted Medea. "Out of my way," she bellowed, brushing past the others to the bedside. Her bulging leather bag hit the floor with a thud.

Medea looked up at the stern face hovering inches above. Her eyes opened wide. "*Circe!* "

"It took me six months to find you," Circe scowled, "but I never thought to see you like this."

Medea tried to speak, but another spasm gripped her.

"We don't know what's wrong," Iole offered timidly. "She just keeps—"

"Get out," Circe barked.

The grandam had been looking on with mounting anger. "See here, who do you think you are?"

"I'm her aunt, you fool," Circe shouted. "Now get out."

"Well, I don't care who you are. We're supposed to—"

Circe leapt up and from the folds of her cloak produced a long, bronze dagger that flashed in the air. "*Out!* " she roared. "Or I'll slice open your fat guts and feed them to the frigging dogs!"

As they scurried from the room, Circe turned back to her niece and with the knife slit the cords that bound her wrists. Gently she laid her hand upon Medea's still swollen belly, then shook her head. "Midwives!" she muttered. "Nitwits." She eyed Euterpe, who had remained behind. "You're her servant?"

"Yes, Ma'am."

"All right. Find a place to put that damn baby down so you can help me." From her leather bag Circe extracted a small vial. "Drink this," she said, putting it to Medea's lips.

Medea drained the potion, then looked despairingly at her aunt. "Am I going to die?"

"Yes, eventually, but not from this."

"Why does it still hurt?"

Circe heaved a sigh. "You can't ever do anything halfway, can you, Niece? You decide to become a mother, and then you insist on having twins!"

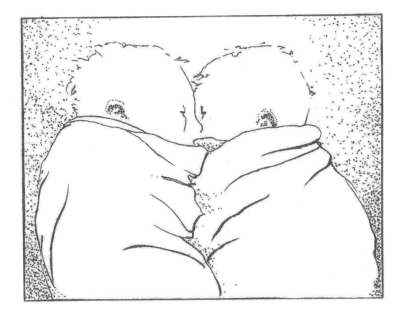

XIX
Promises

JASON COULDN'T BELIEVE IT. *Two boys!* He pumped the messenger's arm, borrowed a horse from Evanus, and galloped home. Medea was sitting up in bed when he arrived, two small, blanketed creatures nestled by her side. He sprang to her, beaming, and hugged her. "Are you all right?"

"Better now, much better. Would you like to hold—?" She paused in confusion, not knowing which child to give him first.

Jason laughed, gingerly lifted the bundle nearest him, cradling it lovingly in his arms. With his finger he brushed the tiny, wrinkled face. "He's so small. He's so ... beautiful." Jason looked from one to the other. "They're both beautiful!"

Medea settled back. "Jason, this is my Aunt Circe. She's come all the way from Aeaea to visit us."

The cloaked figure sitting in the shadows had escaped his notice until now. Jason nodded to the older woman. "I hope you can stay with us for a while."

"No fear of that," Circe commented dryly. "If I'm around

babies too long, I eat them." She slung the leather bag over her shoulder and headed for the door. "Call me when it's dinnertime."

Jason looked at his wife.

"Circe's all right," Medea assured him. "It's just that, she never had any children."

Gently he laid his son back in her arms and gathered up the other boy. "They hardly weigh anything at all. Look at the grip on this guy!" In awe he watched the diminutive hand grasp his finger.

"Would you do me a favor, Jason?"

"Anything."

"Please go after Circe and talk to her, make her feel welcome. It's been years since I've seen her, and right now I can't even get out of bed."

Jason didn't want to leave. He ached to stay here with his wife and his new family, but he said, "Sure." After touching the boy's tiny nose with his own, he returned him to his mother.

It was a cool evening, with some streaks of red still ablaze on the horizon. Jason spotted Circe on a wooden bench across the square. She eyed him as he approached. "It was very good of you to come," he said, forcing a smile. "Medea's told me a lot about you. So, you're from Aeaea. Where exactly is—"

"I won't mince words with you, Jason," she interrupted, her tone icy. "I know what happened back in Colchis."

A chill rose up in him. "What do you mean?"

"Don't screw with me, boy. I know about Apsyrtus."

He swallowed hard. Quietly, firmly he said, "It wasn't me. It was one of my men. I'd give anything for it not to have happened." He paused. "Are you going to tell her?"

"I came here to tell her, and by God I should tell her!" She laid her fist on the bench and gritted her teeth. "But I'm not going to."

Jason watched her. "Why not?"

"Not for you, if that's what you're thinking. I despise you for the coward and the liar that you are. You're too small a man for tragedy, Jason. The problem is, you can cause tragedy for others." Circe looked back toward the house. "The poor fool loves you, and now she's added to her misfortune by bearing your children.

For her sake, I'm going to spare her the truth, and I pray I'm not making a terrible blunder. She tells me you've been a good husband to her."

"I've tried to be."

Circe fixed him with her pitiless dark eyes. "I'm only going to say this once, Jason. Beware. Medea has a mighty soul, far mightier than yours. Tamper with her at your peril."

* * *

Creon held a reception in the palace to honor the birth of Jason's children. At the height of the festivities his daughter threaded her way through the crowded hall to where Medea hovered protectively over the double cradle. "Princess Medea," she said, smoothly extending her hand, "I'm Glauce."

Medea bowed. "Princess."

Glauce smiled down at the small pink faces that peeked out from the bundle of blankets. "Lovely boys, Medea. And their names?"

"This one is Mermerus, and this one Tisander."

"Interesting. The first means 'burdened,' does it not? And the second, 'avenger.' Tell me, why such serious choices?"

"I think it's wrong to give a child a lighthearted, happy name. If he has a sad life, his name will only compound his misery."

"Whereas," Glauce deduced, "if he is lucky enough to enjoy a merry life, he won't mind a solemn name. Very clever, Medea. My own parents chose the middle way. 'Glauce' means owl, which makes one neither happy nor sad."

"Unless one is a field mouse."

A flash of irritation crossed Glauce's features, but she covered it quickly with a laugh. "Very good again, Medea. Jason didn't tell me how quick-witted his wife is. No wonder he spends so little time at the palace anymore."

"He spends little enough time at home either. He can't tear himself away from the project."

"Ah, yes, the road. That's all I hear from my father too these days. A tow road across the isthmus was an ingenious notion, but it took someone with fresh eyes to see how to make it feasible. You must be very proud of your husband. I can see it in your face."

"What can you see?" a booming voice behind her demanded. Creon and Jason huddled now around the cradle.

"I can see," Glauce responded, "that two women cannot enjoy a private chat without a couple of handsome fellows barging in."

Creon tilted his head back in laughter, then smiled at Medea. "Apparently you've met my daughter."

"I introduced myself," Glauce clarified, "since neither you nor Jason can find time to do anything else but talk about your precious highway."

"For your information, we weren't talking shop just now. We were trying to figure out exactly what our family connection was. I know that I'm distantly related to his grandfather, but I can't remember exactly how. I'm sure your dear mother knew, as Jason's mother knows. Women keep much better track of these things than men do."

"It's little wonder," Glauce offered. "After all, it's the women who go through the nuisance of having children. Of course they would keep track of how all those little babies are related." She cast Medea a small, bland smile.

"In any case," Creon continued, "we made scant headway through the ancestral thickets, but never mind. As I was telling Jason, relations be damned! As far as I'm concerned, a man's ability is the only lineage that counts."

Glauce raised an eyebrow. "What a democratic idea!"

"I've been out to the site, and what Jason is accomplishing there is remarkable. The men respect him and work hard for him. Now, it's true that the road may take a bit longer than the year he originally predicted." Creon winked at Jason. "But that's all right. He made that estimate when he was trying to sell me on the idea. I would have done the same thing in his place. The important point is that the job is progressing steadily, and it's all Jason's doing. That to me is more important than any pedigree."

"You're very kind, Sir," Jason said.

Creon turned to him, his tone serious. "You know me better than that. I'm rarely accused of kindness, but most people would grudgingly allow that I am fair. What I'm telling you, Jason, is that kinship may give a man a start, but effort is what determines his future. I've turned away much closer relatives because they had no stomach for work. You are accomplishing things, Jason, and I assure you that your reward will be commensurate with your achievement."

* * *

So occupied was Medea during Circe's brief visit that she scarcely found time to stray from the house. On a rare occasion when both infants slept, she slipped out with Circe long enough to visit the temple and introduce her friend Lyctaea, with whom her crusty aunt enjoyed a curious, almost instant rapport. But for Medea the best thing about Circe's stay was having someone to talk to. All too soon, though, the last day came. Leaving the children in Euterpe's care for a couple of hours, Medea took Circe outside the city gates to a sloping meadow overlooking the gulf. They settled in a patch of wildflowers that waved in the mild spring breezes.

"After you leave tomorrow, Aunt Circe, I'm going to be sorry I spent so much time talking about myself and finding out so little about you. I've often wondered about your life in Aeaea, what your house is like, or your garden. Shall I think of you drying oleander sometimes?"

"You don't need any details," Circe told her. "Whatever you imagine, that's what I'll be doing."

"When you left Colchis, I was sixteen, and I didn't think I'd ever see you again. Now I'm twenty-seven, and this time I know I won't."

"Yes, I won't be visiting anymore, and I don't want you to visit me either. I turn uninvited guests into swine. But have no fear, Medea. We'll live forever, you and I, and this meeting between us will happen again and again."

Medea broke off a blade of grass and pulled it slowly through her fingers. "I know you don't approve of what I've done—I mean, leaving home and marrying Jason, but I was so alone before."

"There are worse things than being alone."

"People said I was mad."

"There are worse things than madness too," she shrugged. "Where's your dagger?"

"I don't need it anymore."

"And what about Hecate? Don't you need her anymore either? No prayers, no libations, no sacrifices. I made you a votaress when I left Colchis, and you promised to continue her worship."

"She scares me now."

"She's supposed to scare you. She's a goddess of the Underworld." From her leather bag Circe drew out a wineskin. "Do you still know the prayer?"

"Of course I do, but—"

"Good. Humor me."

Medea pulled the stopper from the skin. Her eyes closed, the familiar words floated back. Quietly she chanted, "*Hecate can heal. Hecate can harm. Hecate can breed. Hecate can blight.*" She let the wine flow to the ground. Then each took a small sip in turn.

"I feel like a hypocrite," Medea confessed, handing back the skin. "I'm no longer certain Hecate even exists."

"The gods don't expect certainty from us. They reserve that for themselves. What they expect is loyalty."

"Loyalty?"

"Loyalty is the cardinal human virtue. Don't ever forget that, Medea."

She looked at Circe. "I'm so grateful that you came. I wish—"

"Stop. Sentimentality doesn't suit you. If you want to show gratefulness, promise your old aunty something."

"Anything."

"Remember Hecate."

XX
Spring of Peirene

JASON LOVED HIS SONS more than anything. Medea watched him cuddle them in his lap, one at a time or both together, rock them tirelessly when he came home in the evening, some nights falling asleep himself while they dozed in his arms. Jason's fierce attachment to the boys should have pleased her, but she also found it unsettling somehow. Why was her love for them never quite so simple, so wholehearted as his? When she bathed Mermerus, tender affection welled up in her, but also a strange uneasiness. As Tisander sucked eagerly upon her breast, she looked on with a mixture of awe and abhorrence. That she should be milked like a goat was revolting to her, but also alluring, as there is some allure in all revolting things.

But what distressed Medea more was the change in Jason, subtle at first. Their lovemaking was not the same as before. A vague, intangible barrier seemed to have dropped between them. Usually so open, so talkative in his rambling style, Jason had become reserved and distant. Medea told herself that it was merely his preoccupation with the road. When it was done, their intimacy would return. When it was done, she would have him back again.

* * *

Full summer now oppressed Corinth, hot, airless, and inescapable. As the sun beat mercilessly on the shimmering isthmus, a lone figure clipped along briskly, her sandals tapping on the brand new surface. She encountered no one until nearly halfway across, and then arose a din of shouting and ringing hammers, and a dust cloud from the bustling activity. Men threw up shovelfuls of dirt in the long, wide trench. Others with rakes graded the roadbed. Still others strained to haul carts piled high with stone. As one group of workers after another caught sight of her, they paused to offer a respectful bow to the king's daughter, which Glauce acknowledged with a nod.

She spotted Jason in conversation with his foreman. He had one hand on Evanus's back, and with the other pointed in the direction of the open sea. As Evanus trudged off, Jason turned and saw her. "Princess!"

"Father kept telling me that I absolutely had to come and see what you're up to."

She wore a gleaming white chiton, and Jason noted the pearl droplets of sweat that slid down from her throat and disappeared beneath the thin material. "You picked a very hot day to visit, Princess."

"Nonsense. If I'd waited for a cool day, I would have had to wait until fall, and at the rate you're going, you'll be finished by then."

"I wish that were so, Princess."

"Tell me what insurmountable problems you're solving today."

He smiled, looked toward the sea again. "A boulder, a big one, right in our path. If we don't move it before tonight, it'll halt the whole operation tomorrow."

"Why not just go around it?"

Jason shook his head. "The road must be absolutely straight. Curves, even slight ones, will hinder portage."

Richard Matturro

"I see. Very clever." She surveyed the work site. "Those men over there," she said, indicating a small group crouching in the roadbed and chipping at blocks of stone. "What are they doing?"

"They're stone fitters. There are six of them, and they're the most skilled craftsmen I have. Their job is to fit the paving tightly." He pressed his two hands together to demonstrate. "The tighter the stones, the smoother the surface will be. If the road is a success, it will be because of those half-dozen men."

Glauce gave him a knowing look. "Don't play modest with me, Jason. Their skill notwithstanding, if the road is a success, it will be because of you."

"Thank you, Princess."

"Now, Jason, the other reason for my visit. I'm to fetch you back for dinner at the palace. Father wants to talk to you about draft horses. Do you know anything about draft horses?"

"No, nothing."

"Entirely too honest an answer, Jason. I see you're not quite ready for a life of public service. Father has been offered eight teams at a fairly good price, and he wants to discuss their suitability for towing ships. If you'll take my advice, you'll just encourage him to buy the lot. That's what he wants to do anyway, but he'll feel so much better about it if you back him up."

Jason laughed. "I guess I can manage that. Tell him I'll come as soon as we're done for the day."

"Not a bit of it. You'll come right now."

"But I can't, Princess. I have to—"

She raised a small, lovely hand. "I'm sorry, you're being ordered."

"By the king?"

"No, by me. You've barely left this infernal thoroughfare since you began. No one, Jason, no matter what degree of genius he may aspire to, is indispensable. Please notify your very able foreman that you're taking the rest of the day off."

* * *

The pavement burned under his feet, and the air was stifling, but Jason didn't notice. The more she asked him about the project, the more animated he became. As they headed back toward town, he told her how he loved the challenge, the chance to lead so many men in a united effort, the opportunity to make Corinth the first city in Greece, and Glauce seemed to share his enthusiasm. Jason had walked this road a hundred times now, but it had never seemed so bright, so golden. Occasionally he would catch the scent of her perspiration, a perfume that made her seem appealingly vulnerable.

Too soon they reached the city gates. "Well," Jason said, looking at his dusty hands, "if I'm going to see the king, I'd better go home and clean up first."

"Do you know the Spring of Peirene?"

"No."

"It's in the lower city. They say it was formed on the very spot where the winged horse, Pegasus, pounded his hoof. Come along," she said, grabbing his arm. "You can wash there." She led him past the market square, then threaded through a tangle of winding streets past abandoned workshops, decaying storehouses, to the very oldest part of town. At the bottom of a crumbling stairway she pushed open a creaking wooden door and peeked inside. "Good! No one's here."

Jason found himself in a cavernous stone grotto, cool even at midday. The dim interior was interrupted by thin shafts of sunlight admitted through crevices in the ceiling. A low, uneven shelf surrounded the dark pool. Noise of the city had died away. Inside, all Jason could hear was the silvery tinkle of water dripping from the cave walls.

Glauce slipped off her sandals and dipped a toe in the water. "It's perfect," she declared. Drawing the jeweled pins, she shook her head, letting her hair fall down her back. Then she untied her waist cord and removed the broaches from her shoulders. The chiton dropped to the floor. Without a backward glance she dove in.

Jason stood for a moment. Hesitantly he shed his own tunic, then took a deep breath and followed her. The water was

Richard Matturro

shockingly cold after the intense heat of the day. Jason bobbed to the surface and gasped for air.

At the far end of the pool Glauce was watching him, only her head visible above the surface. "Your hair looks as bad as mine does when it's wet!" she laughed.

Indeed, it was startling to see her elegant brown swirls, now many shades darker, plastered down the sides of her face like a peasant. Yet somehow it only added to her charm. The narrow shafts of sunlight reflected a rippling pattern throughout the dome and danced over her features. Jason took another breath and slid beneath the surface. He emerged several feet from her.

"Which side of the family do your curls come from?" Glauce asked.

"My mother's side," he said as he watched her bathe her arms and her legs.

"There's no curly hair on either side of my family. Father jokes that on his side, there's no hair at all. Do you worry about losing yours someday, Jason?"

"I never thought much about it."

"Well, I can't understand men worrying about such a thing. I don't think it detracts from one's appearance at all." She dipped her hands into the water again and splashed her face. "Wonderful, isn't it?"

"It is, Princess."

She looked at him. "You know, you're really going to have to stop this inane formality. After all, you're descended from royalty just like I am. Do you think you can bring yourself to call me Glauce?"

He smiled. "I'll try ... Glauce."

"A valiant start."

She braced her hands on the ledge and lifted herself up, her feet dangling in the pool. Jason rubbed the remaining dust from his limbs, then hauled himself upon the ledge as well. He was careful to sit a discrete distance away, but he could not help stealing glances at her naked body, so different from Medea's. Though slender, she had none of his wife's angularity or odd boyishness, and her skin was so light, so smooth, so—. Jason turned away. "How did the spring get its name?" he asked.

"It's a sad story. Long ago on her way back from Lechaeum, Peirene learned that her son had been killed by the goddess Artemis. She was so distraught that she drowned herself here. Can you imagine killing yourself out of grief? I love my father, and I'll certainly grieve when he dies, but I can't imagine killing myself. Of course it must be different when one has children, as you do, and a wife."

"It's very different." Jason made a small whirlpool with his heel and stared down into the vortex. "I'd do anything for my boys."

Glauce leaned back and closed her eyes. "It must have been terribly romantic, to be on a quest in a wild, foreign land, and meet an exotic princess. I've heard all kinds of outlandish stories about the Colchians. Some even say they practice human sacrifice. Is that true?"

"Of course not, but they have some curious customs."

"So do we, I suppose. And do they all speak with the same accent—like Medea does?"

"Yes, more or less."

"I wonder if your two sons will pick it up."

Jason frowned and was silent.

"They probably won't," Glauce concluded. "Children tend to speak like the other children they meet no matter how their parents talk. Your twins will probably end up with the same dull speech as the rest of us."

"Your speech isn't dull, Glauce."

She flashed him a smile. "I do believe, Jason, that this is a milestone. After spending nearly a year in Corinth and talking with me on numerous occasions, you have finally seen fit to pay me your first compliment: my speech isn't dull."

Laughing, he tried to protest, but Glauce merely patted his knee and slid into the pool. "Come on, Jason, time for one more dip before we return to the palace and discuss draft horses."

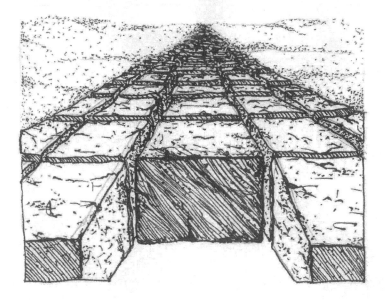

XXI
First City

WITH AUTUMN the rains came once again, slowing progress on the road more than the chill of winter or the heat of summer. His men standing idle, Jason leaned in the doorway of the shed and cursed the downpour as it turned the work site into a lake of mud. At home he was irritable and peevish, snapped at Medea when his dinner was cold. Other times he sat silently at the table, brooding. Only his sons escaped his displeasure, and Medea found herself envying her own children for the affection he continued to lavish on them. When the rainy season finally passed and the mud dried, Jason redoubled his efforts on the project. During his rare hours with his family, he seemed reluctant to look Medea full in the face. At best, he was simply polite. At worst he was—not hostile, not even angry—just absent.

By late winter he'd pressed the highway to within sight of the Saronic Sea, striking distance of completion, and Creon designated the spring equinox for the laying of the final stone. When that day arrived, a citywide holiday was proclaimed, and the people of Corinth streamed down to the harbor to see the marvel that had been wrought.

Festooned with ribbons, the royal barge lay just offshore, ready to embark on its singular voyage. In front of a stone slab on the beach, Creon called upon Zeus to bless the city's endeavor, and he doused the altar with wine in honor of Aphrodite, Corinth's patron deity. But when the white ram was led forward for sacrifice, his final prayer was to Poseidon, the jealous god of the sea, whose two watery domains the road would connect.

From his place at the rudder, Evanus signaled the rowers to ease the barge toward shore where two teams of horses, each a brace of stout geldings, thumped impatiently. As the ship touched ground, they were quickly brought up on either side and hitched to cleats low under the bow. Presently the ship's crew scrambled over the side to lighten the load. Then the horses dug in, straining against the harnesses. With a snap the ropes stretched taut, and the barge, scraping along the sand, rose dripping from the water and slid onto the smooth rollers in the new stone passage. An amazed buzz arose from the spectators.

Then began the strangest pageant in living memory. The swaying vessel, trailing ten thousand clamorous citizens in its wake, rumbled overland in a dry canal. Four miles and four hours later this curious procession came to a halt near the edge of the plateau overlooking the Saronic Sea. Waves of onlookers, like two wings, folded forward now on both sides of the road and jockeyed for a view of the two-foot-square gap in the pavement.

The six stone fitters had been here since daybreak. Now, their moment come, they strained to heft the last block and carry it onto the roadbed where Jason and Evanus waited. Carefully they lowered it, levering with wedges, until it settled neatly, almost seamlessly, into place. Jason caught his foreman's eye. The road was complete.

But now came the trickiest maneuver of all. Fresh teams of horses were hitched to the stern of the barge. Cautiously the ship inched over the edge of the plateau onto the ramp. While the rear teams struggled to keep the barge from careening down the slope,

Richard Matturro

the forward horses were unhitched and drawn off. Jason held his breath. Slowly, haltingly, its mast pitching from side to side, the barge was lowered toward the beach. Then, with a great splash the bow plunged into the water. When the ship was seen to bob and float freely once more in its natural element, a wild, ecstatic shout went up from the crowd.

Evanus had remained by Jason's side. He shuffled shyly now, then thrust out a brown hand toward his chief. Jason smiled, brushed the hand aside, and hugged his startled foreman.

* * *

It did not take long for neighboring cities on the gulf to recognize the value of the tow road. Whether portage took four hours in good weather or eight hours in bad, it so surpassed the tedious sea voyage around the Peloponnese that it was deemed worth the fee that Corinth levied. By midsummer, ships were regularly backed up at Lechaeum waiting for passage, and there was already talk of enlarging the harbor and widening the road. Between the duty exacted and the increased mercantile traffic, Corinth was becoming a rich city. Within a year, it had recouped all that had been spent building the road. In two years the treasury had doubled. Jason, meanwhile, had grown into Creon's most trusted adviser.

During these same two years, Medea's transformation was more subtle. Fate may have picked her out for a uniquely tragic role, but it led her there by an unheroic path a million other women had trod. Medea raised the twins largely by herself, despite their father's devotion. Mermerus's first words were babbled in her ear. Tisander's first unsteady steps were taken while holding her hand. She wiped their noses, picked their vomit from her clothes. She became accustomed to smells that once would have made her gag. She learned to tolerate shrieking that would have shattered her eardrums if not her nerves. And while she paced this dull landscape of trite horrors, she watched Jason fall out of love with her.

Dignity in the face of heartache is usually deemed courageous, but such courage is often merely the accidental valor of postponement. Like many before and since, Medea put off her dread. Such tactics take their toll. When verity is ignored in one place, it can be overlooked in all places. Last of all, one's own verity may be lost.

Even as she dodged some truths, though, Medea unexpectedly stumbled upon another. She made the homely discovery that time passes indiscriminately. Events, momentous or trivial, slip into the past with equal languor. First a day went by, then a week, and so on, until she found to her dismay that she had been living for years with something she thought she could not bear for an hour.

* * *

Jason strode across the courtyard. He was accustomed to being summoned to the palace and rarely felt butterflies in his stomach anymore. He found the king in his private quarters, hands clasped behind his back, gazing out the window toward the harbor.

"Sir, you wanted to see me?"

Creon turned, but his thoughts seemed somewhere else. "Jason, please sit down." Slowly Creon stepped over to the table and filled two bronze goblets, then pulled his own chair closer. After an uncomfortable silence, he said, "Jason, I have a reputation for being frank, as you know, but the subject I need to speak of requires delicacy, not frankness. There's a lot at stake, so forgive me if I'm not as tactful as I would like." He paused. "It's common knowledge that your marriage is no longer happy."

Jason felt the blood rush to his face.

"Ordinarily, this would be no concern of mine. A man's private life is his own affair. You've done good service for me, and that's all that matters."

"May I ask what the problem is, Sir?"

"That will become clear in a moment, but before I go further, I must hear it from your own lips. Have you thought about leaving Medea?"

Jason averted his eyes. "I've tried ... *not* to think about it."

The king nodded. "Marriage between a Greek and a foreigner is difficult. We have an unfair tendency to consider all outlanders as barbarians, but there are differences that are impossible to ignore, and that's why such marriages are discouraged. I don't say this to criticize. You were a young man when you married. You're still a young man. When I was young, God knows I did things I blush at now. But that's neither here nor there." He set down his cup deliberately. "When you first came to Corinth, I had doubts about your ability, and even now you have many things to learn, but one of your best attributes, Jason, is your willingness to make mistakes, to fall down and get right up again wiser than before. I also like the fairness with which you treat those under you. The talent to be both obeyed and respected is rare in a man. You have foresightedness, boldness, and perseverance. These are the qualities of a successful leader."

"Thank you, Sir, but what does my marriage have to do with this?"

Creon sighed, ran his palm over the rim of his goblet. "I have no son, as you know. It's the one misfortune of my life. But I've been blessed with a daughter whom I love very much. My other love is this glorious city, and it's Corinth that's in jeopardy. Without a son, I leave the succession uncertain." Creon folded his hands now and leveled his gaze. "Jason, I'll come right to the point. Nothing would please me more than if you would consent to marry Glauce and, when I die, succeed me as king."

Jason's mouth went dry.

"From my perspective," Creon continued, "such a marriage would be ideal. I dispose of both my daughter and my city at a stroke, and to a man I trust." He picked up his wine again and took a long draft, then paused for a while peering at his companion. "Well, what do you have to say?"

"Sir, I'm ... quite certain I'm the wrong man."

Jason heard Creon's booming laugh again. "Some of my council will doubtless agree with you, but never mind. Let them bellyache. None of them could have done what you've done. Don't worry, Jason. You'll grow into the job just as I did, and I have confidence that you'll be no worse in it than I was. Maybe better. And with luck I'll have years to prepare you for it."

Desperately needing to move, Jason rose now, crossed the room—walked away from Creon, but he could not walk away from the thoughts careening through his brain. Finally, more to himself than the other, he asked, "How does the princess feel about this?"

"How the princess feels is of no consequence," Creon snapped imperiously. After a moment he snorted, then softened his tone. "To set your mind at rest, I've sounded her out, and she's not exactly adverse to marrying you."

Without turning around Jason asked, "What happens to Medea?"

"It would be best if she left Corinth."

"To go where?"

"That's entirely up to her," Creon shrugged. "Back to her own country, I should think."

"No," Jason said, speaking low, "they won't have her back."

"Well, somewhere else then. In any case, we have no intention of being unfair to her. She'll have ample means to settle wherever she likes. She and the children will want for nothing."

Jason spun around. "The children?"

"They will go with their mother, of course."

"No, Sir, that's impossible. I can't send my boys away."

"This is difficult, Jason, I know. But let me remind you of why it's essential. Having no male heir, I have no indisputable successor. The nobility will accept you if they're assured that the royal line will continue through Glauce. In other words, they must be certain that it's a son of you and my daughter—not of you and a foreigner—who will eventually rule."

"I understand that, Sir, but I still can't do it."

"This isn't for my benefit, Jason. Your sons present no threat to me. The threat will be to you and to civic order once you're king. If they're allowed to remain in Corinth, every malcontent will pin his hopes on them. Nobles, members of your own council might turn against you and form a faction with one of your sons. Nothing undermines a peaceful succession like rivals to the throne. They must leave."

Jason stood silent for a long moment, then took a deep breath. Slowly, evenly he said, "I appreciate your faith in me, Sir, but I can't accept your offer. I will not exile my own sons."

Creon lowered his eyes. He set his cup down, then slowly rose and passed to the window once again. The air tingled in the room, and Jason was left to listen to the sound of his own breathing. After an almost interminable pause, Creon said quietly, "I hate striving with a man who I know in my heart is wrong. But even more," he added, "I hate striving with a man who I know is right."

Jason looked at him.

"You're a better man than I thought," Creon said, turning around. "I couldn't exile a child of mine either. This is going to make things harder, much harder. If we can't bar them by exile, we'll have to do it by law. Swear a solemn oath that your sons by Medea are excluded from the succession. God knows, you may live to regret this decision. A law is only as good as the men who are called upon to observe it, but I don't see any other alternative if the boys are to stay." He stopped, eyed Jason. "Is that agreeable to you? An oath that they won't succeed you?"

"Yes, of course."

"Does that mean you accept my offer?"

Jason hesitated. This was the moment, this time and this place, and he didn't even know how he got here. He focused on the older man standing across the room and heard himself say, "Yes."

"Good man."

XXII
Verity

SHE WAS THINKING OF CERBERUS, the triple-headed dog who guards the gates of the Underworld. It was a game Jason played. He would perch one boy on each shoulder, then growl ferociously and bare his teeth while they squealed with delight.

Medea held Mermerus a little tighter on her lap while Tisander crawled under the table. Though twins, they were different really. Tisander was more independent, more adventurous. Perhaps he would seek his own Golden Fleece one day. Mermerus was more thoughtful, a touch shy, which made Medea feel protective of him. What would he become? A poet? A sculptor? A builder?

The door swung open and Euterpe marched in, her basket under one arm. "It's mackerel again, Madam," she announced disgustedly. "I hope you don't mind. It was a choice between that and cuttlefish, and I know how the master feels about cuttlefish." She eyed the twins. "Have they been behaving themselves?"

"Exceptionally—today."

"My sister's got a two-year-old, and I don't mind telling you

Richard Matturro

that Pelorus is a little terror compared to them." She mopped her forehead with her sleeve. "I'd better see to these fish. In this heat, they're not going to keep."

At that moment the door opened again, and Jason appeared in the entry. His children flew to him, each snagging a leg. He clumped in, giving them a ride.

"You're early," Medea said.

Crouching, he tousled Mermerus's fine hair and chucked Tisander under the chin, then looked up at Euterpe. "Can you take them out for a while?"

"I did take them out this morning, Sir."

"Take them out again, Euterpe."

She set the basket down. "Yes, Sir."

Medea watched him closely as he shut the door behind them. When he turned back again, his eyes sought hers—for the first time, it seemed, in years. Suddenly there was a gnawing deep in her gut.

"I need to talk to you," he said.

"What about?"

He took a breath. "There's no good way, so I'm just going to say it. Creon spoke to me. He's ... chosen me to succeed him."

"Succeed him—as king?"

"Yes." Jason bit his lip. "There's more. He's determined that I should be accepted as his heir. We're connected by blood, as you know, but only distantly."

"Well, there's not much he can do about that. He can't make you into a closer relation."

"There is one way: by making me a son-in-law." He added, "By marrying me to Glauce."

For the briefest moment Medea felt the urge to laugh. "But you're already married."

"Yes, he knows that, and he also knows, as you and I both know, that there isn't much of a marriage left between us."

And now silence descended upon them as the import of his words sank in. Medea searched his familiar features, but found only a resolute mask. "Jason," she said slowly, "you can't do this.

I gave up everything for you—my family, my home."

"It's not as one-sided as you make it out to be. You left Colchis of your own free will. I took you out of a backward country where you were treated like an imbecile."

She shook her head, tried to focus on something: the table, the floor, the basket of fish in the corner. "Do you love her?"

His voice registered irritation. "Creon is arranging this marriage for dynastic reasons—nothing more."

"So you're saying you don't love her?"

"I'm saying that love never entered into it. People don't get married just for love, especially king's daughters."

"I'm a king's daughter," she reminded him, her voice cracking, "and I did. But then I'm from a backward country, and an imbecile besides."

"Medea—"

"Do you love her?"

"Listen, I told you—"

"What is it you love about her, Jason? Is it her eyes, because they're straighter than mine? Is it her hair? Or is it her mouth, and the perfect little words she says?"

"Stop it!"

"Why don't you tell me the truth, Jason? What beautiful thing is it about beautiful Glauce that you love?"

"All right!" he shouted. "You want to know what I love about her? I love that she has a light heart, where everything isn't laden with deep meaning. She's a happy person, and she's interested in things, practical things." Jason drew breath to say more, then shook his head, as if to dispel the anger. After a moment he sighed heavily and slumped into the chair across the table from her. When he spoke again, his tone was softer. "I'm sorry, Medea. I don't want to hurt you. I never intended for it to turn out like this. You have to believe me."

Distantly she inquired, "What happens now?"

"Creon wants you to leave Corinth. That wasn't my choice, but all your needs will be taken care of." Jason paused. "He wanted the boys to go too, but I talked him into allowing them to stay."

A dark thing seized her throat. "No, you wouldn't. You wouldn't take my children from me."

"Medea, I can offer them a better life here. You know that. Their own father is going to be king."

"You don't understand. It took me so long to *become* their mother. I don't care what you do with me, or where you send me, but you can't take them away. Think about what you're doing."

"I have thought about it. It wasn't easy to convince Creon. We're lucky he's a reasonable man."

"Reasonable? To separate a mother from her children? You call that reasonable? You call it lucky?"

"He has been reasonable, believe me. But if you make trouble, he could easily change his mind. I don't want to try his patience."

"*His* patience!" Her fists slammed the table, and she was on her feet, her face inches from his. "*What about my patience?*" she roared as he backed away. "You're going to marry another woman, take my children from me, and send me into exile, and you're worrying about *his* patience? *Damn you, Jason!* Damn you for the spineless, wretched thing that you are." She glared at him a moment longer, then fell back into the chair. Her hands covering her face, she heaved in noiseless sobs while the little room seemed to collapse upon her, buried under a thousand years of dust and rubble. Minutes passed. Then, from somewhere, far away, she heard her own voice ask, "Do you remember sleeping in the rain?"

"I remember," he said quietly.

"We didn't know where we were going, what we were going to do, but we had each other, and the whole world ahead of us." Barely audible she pleaded, "Jason, I have no one, no friends, no family. I beg you, don't take my children."

His chair scraped as he pushed it back. "Creon's given me a place in the palace," he said. "The wedding is a week from today. That will give you time to settle your affairs and make arrangements for where you'd like to go. The boys can stay here until you leave. Needless to say, if there's any way I can help, I will."

She looked up. He was standing at the door.

"Good-bye, Medea."

* * *

The city was humming with anticipation of the royal nuptials. Daily at the palace workmen arrived to prepare the great hall, while carts weighed down with fabrics and delicacies were wheeled into the courtyard. By contrast Medea's home remained quiet, unhurried. She continued to go about her normal business as if nothing had changed. Early in the morning, two days before the wedding, Euterpe was surprised by a knock on the door. She told the caller to wait.

"Madam, there's a Lyctaea—from the *temple*—to see you."

Medea was helping Mermerus on with his tunic. "Show her in."

Euterpe stepped aside to let her pass. Then, with a disapproving backward glance, she herded the children into another room.

"I hope you don't mind my coming," Lyctaea said.

"Sit down."

Lyctaea pulled a chair close to hers and touched her arm. "I heard the news. I'm so sorry. Do you know what you're going to do yet, where you're going to go?"

"No."

"It's unfair what they're doing to you. I don't see how—"

"Please tell me why you're here." Her tone was calm, reserved.

Lyctaea apologized. "I don't mean to intrude. As much as I wanted to see you, I would never have barged in like this if I hadn't promised your aunt."

Medea's eyes snapped up. "My aunt?"

"Before she left Corinth, Circe came back to the temple to talk with me—alone. She told me something, and then made me vow, before Aphrodite and Hecate, that I'd never reveal it unless Jason … did something like this."

"Reveal what?"

Lyctaea inhaled deeply. "I hate to be the one who has to tell you. It's your brother."

"Apsyrtus? What about him?"

"That evening, back in Colchis, when Jason stole the Golden Fleece, your brother was there in the temple. He'd gone to stand guard overnight." She paused. "They killed him."

A veil slid over Medea's face, and her crossed eyes glimpsed him. Apsyrtus was smiling his silly, charming, boyish smile. Always joking, always idle, so good-hearted. He was probably trying to be a hero that night. He didn't know the butchers he was dealing with. But they weren't to blame. They hadn't killed him really. She had, as much as if she'd wielded the knife herself. Apsyrtus—the poor fool had been looking forward to his wedding, and now—Medea's lips tightened. Now it was her husband looking forward to his.

"If there's anything I can do—"

Medea blinked, focused on Lyctaea again. "Thank you, no. It's up to me now."

* * *

The contest in her soul was uneven from the start, the conclusion foregone. A divinity, older, darker, mightier claimed dominion. As Medea sat by herself, there was no visible sign when the battle was finally lost, when the last redoubt fell. Imperceptibly, as one drifts from wakefulness to sleep, the ground shifted. One instant she was merely another woman who had been wronged. The next she became the woman who would requite all such wrongs since the world began.

There was stirring in the next room. Euterpe appeared at the door. "Has she left?"

Medea rose and retrieved her leather bag off a high shelf. "I'm going out," she said as she searched through it. "While I'm gone, please send for my horse."

"Yes, Madam."

She slipped something into the folds of her chiton. "I won't be long."

XXIII
Cardinal Human Virtue

IN HER MIRROR Glauce saw the guard approach, apprehension on his youthful features. "What is it?" she asked.

"Excuse me, my lady, but there's someone to see you."

"Yes?"

"It's ... the Princess Medea."

A chill went through her. "What does she want?"

"She didn't say, my lady."

Glauce frowned, put the mirror back on her dressing table. "All right. Bring her up, but stay within call."

"Yes, my lady."

Why come here? Why even show her face? Glauce stood, adjusted one of the pins in her hair. She assumed a grave demeanor as Medea was shown in.

"Princess Glauce," she said, bowing, "thank you for seeing me."

"I needn't tell you, Medea, that this comes as a surprise."

"Forgive me, Princess. If urgency did not demand it, I wouldn't disturb you at such a time."

"Well?"

"King Creon has determined that my sons are to remain here in Corinth after I leave. Princess, I know you have influence with the king. I ask you to use it now to reverse that decision."

So that's all she wants. Glauce was relieved. "We are not cruel, Medea. It was never my wish or my father's to separate you from your sons. It is Jason who wants them to stay."

"I know that, Princess, and I don't blame you or the king for this. I don't even blame Jason. But I appeal to you as a woman because you understand the bond between a mother and her children."

"Though I sympathize, of course, you're asking me to go against the wishes of the man who will be my husband."

"In the long run this will benefit him, Princess. If the gods bless you with children, Mermerus and Tisander will envy them. Only calamity can result."

Glauce turned back to her dressing table. "That possibility has crossed my mind, but to thwart Jason in this would cause him much distress."

"In my country, Princess, we have a proverb: medicine must taste ill to do good."

"Indeed." Glauce drummed her fingers in thought. "When do you plan to leave Corinth?"

"At break of day tomorrow, Princess."

Glauce stood a moment longer, then faced Medea again and found those disquieting eyes staring crookedly at her. "I can give you no assurances, but I will speak with my father."

"Thank you, Princess."

When Medea still lingered, Glauce asked, "Is there something else?"

"Princess, would you make a libation?"

"I have already promised I would plead on your behalf," she said, annoyance in her voice. "You have no need to bind me with an oath."

"No, Princess, but it is customary to pray the gods' help in a difficult endeavor."

"Very well," Glauce muttered. From the pitcher she poured two small cups of wine and handed one to Medea. Closing her eyes and bowing her head she intoned, "Lady Aphrodite, all praises of Corinth fly up to you, all blessings rain down upon us. If it please you, speed my effort to aid Medea in her request." Glauce spilt a drop, and both women drank.

Medea put down her cup. "Now my success is certain."

For the first time in the interview, she had failed to use Glauce's title, and on the way out she also failed to bow. Curious behavior for someone asking a favor, Glauce thought. Nevertheless, she would help Medea, if only because in this circumstance their two interests coincided. Jason's brats by a foreigner had no business in Corinth. How to banish them, though, without alienating her husband-to-be, that was the problem. It would take some forethought, some extreme delicacy, but it could be done. Glauce smiled. After all, she was her father's daughter.

Glauce sat at her dressing table again. What on earth had Jason ever seen in the woman? Oh, she had a kind of rough, exotic beauty, yes, but her features were so dark, and her eyes—. Glauce shuddered, remembering her unnatural stare. As she reached for her mirror, the first pain hit her. She grimaced, her hands clutching her stomach. What was it? Something she ate? Something she drank? Glimpsing the empty cup of wine, a horrifying thought shot through her. She stood abruptly, toppling the chair, as a hot fluid rose in her throat. She coughed to clear it, but gagged instead as another spasm doubled her over. Staggering, she tried to heave, but her mouth filled with a foul-tasting foam. The guard! Was he still there? If she could reach the door. Groaning she made a rush for it, but a convulsion knocked her sideways. She grabbed for her dressing table, but snagged only the mirror, which she pulled to the floor.

Folded up like a newborn, she jerked uncontrollably, the foam oozing from her lips. All the while she gripped the mirror close to her face, but her eyes, already rolled back into her skull, saw other things. A little dog she'd had when she was five years old barked at her heels, but now it bore Jason's face. Her father leaned over her bed and cried, his tears burning her flesh. The last thing she saw before her heart gave out was an owl, blind and fettered, towed over the portage road by a field mouse.

* * *

The mare was tied up outside, Euterpe waiting at the door. "The boys have been fed, Madam, and they're taking their nap."

"Thank you, Euterpe. Jason is down at Lechaeum today. Would you please fetch him home?"

"Yes, Madam."

"Tell him he's wanted at the palace first. Then you can take the rest of the day off."

"Of course, Madam." She hesitated, her face drawn in sadness.

"What is it, Euterpe?"

"Will I ... not see you again?"

"No," Medea said quietly. "I'm leaving Corinth today."

"I just want to—" her voice broke. She lowered her eyes, brushed them with a rough hand. "I'm sorry to see you go."

Euterpe hurried off. Medea watched her until she disappeared around the corner, and even then Medea remained, as if fixed to the threshold, unwilling to go further. Slowly she entered the house and closed the door behind her. Her eyes lit on the leather bag, which lay where she had dropped it on the table. Reaching inside she felt for the bronze dagger, still swathed in cloth. She unwrapped it, held it in her palm, and felt her fingers curl naturally, almost lovingly, around the smooth, molded hilt. She took a deep breath and stepped into the next room.

The twins lay curled up on their sides, Tisander snuggled behind, his little arm wrapped around Mermerus's waist, his nose tucked into his brother's nape. Medea brushed a wisp of hair from Mermerus's forehead. In sleep he stirred.

There was but one way—quickly, without thinking about it. First one boy, then the other. Gently she tilted Tisander's head back away from his brother and slid the keen edge next to his throat. She knew well enough how to do it, mercifully and almost painlessly. She had done it countless times with animals. She gazed down at Tisander's placid features.

Figs. Euterpe had been teaching him how to peel figs last week. Hunched over the table he dug his nails into the plump, purple fruit, frustrated because he could not separate the skin without tearing the meat inside. At the time Medea half-expected him to bawl in frustration, and was ready to gather him up and comfort him, but then to her surprise he had presented to her a perfect peeled fig, perfect as the small fingers that grasped it, and he gave it to her—a gift.

Medea's hand trembled. "I can't," she whispered. "It is beyond me."

But the old image rose up, the featureless, dark goddess, enthroned in the red chambers of her heart. Beyond you? Your sinews were twisted and hardened when the earth began. The fire that courses through your veins burned before time. Beyond you? *Nothing* is beyond you.

She clenched the dagger.

Fail and a new, indifferent dawn finds you gone, your age past. The moment is yours, this moment, now, to be gaped at in horror across the centuries. Now. Now. *Now!*

Her elbow jerked.

And the world changed.

The knife was still in her hand, a thin film of blood upon the blade. The wound was expert—long, deep, sufficient—and from it Tisander's blood spewed upon the bed, upon his brother's back. But that's not what woke Mermerus. In his death throes, Tisander's legs flew out violently, kicking his brother. Eyes now opened wide, Mermerus found his mother leaning over him, a dripping dagger in her hand, and then the appalling red gash in his brother's neck. Mermerus shrieked.

"You could not spare me this," were the words she now pronounced to the deaf gods. Roughly Medea pinned her son to the bed with her left hand. For a moment the dagger hovered above his squirming body until the thin point touched the very center of his chest. Then she plunged it home. With a hideous crack it split the boy's tender breastbone on its way to his heart.

Mermerus quivered under his mother's hand, his blood spurting onto her face, onto her chiton. It soaked the bed linen joining that of his brother, forming a widening red pool. He twitched a moment longer, then ceased moving forever.

* * *

Euterpe wandered among the stalls in the market, uneasy, taking little note of the stacks of bread or caged chickens. She had delivered the message to Jason over an hour ago, but now could find no enjoyment in her afternoon off. Perhaps on second thought Medea might need her at home, to help her pack, or to mind the boys.

"So, you like it?" a voice asked. The bearded merchant gestured toward the bolt of fine wool in her hands.

Euterpe put it down. "No. I mean, yes. I need to think about it."

It was a long, steep climb from the market square, and Euterpe was out of breath when she finally reached the upper city. She was still puffing when she turned onto her own street and saw the throng gathered outside her home. Then she heard the unearthly howl, the cry of a soul in agony. Euterpe pushed her way through the onlookers and rushed inside. The little apartment was crowded with somber faces, the king's soldiers, who would have stopped her, but she shoved past them to the twins' room.

The boys lay in a sea of red, Jason's heaving frame sprawled over them. Euterpe cried out, and suddenly felt herself slammed against the wall, Jason's hands painfully gripping her upper arms. "*Where is she?*" he demanded.

Euterpe gasped, unable to speak.

"Your mistress!" he roared, his eyes bulging, his breath hot in her face. "She did this."

"No, Sir! She couldn't have!"

"She did, you fool! First Glauce, then ... *this*."

"No—not her own children."

Savagely Jason dug in his nails into her flesh and nearly lifted her off the floor. "Her clothes, her bloody clothes are in the next room. The bloody bitch changed her clothes while her children ... *my* children—" He choked. "*Where is she?*"

"I don't know, Sir. She called for her horse. She said she was leaving Corinth. That's all I know."

For a moment Euterpe thought her own life would end now too, and barely cared if it did, but slowly the strength drained from Jason's arms. He loosened his grip and collapsed to his knees, burying his face in the bed. Tears burning her cheeks, Euterpe slowly approached and looked down at the two small bodies she had cared for since their birth.

"My boys!" Jason sobbed. "My boys! My beautiful boys!"

Richard Matturro

XXIV
Sanctuary

AEGEUS WAS ROCKING the child on his knee when he heard his friend wheezing outside the door. "Come in, Gration," he called.

A large, untidy figure with shaggy gray hair labored in. When he reached the table, he laid a thick hand heavily upon it to steady himself.

"For God's sake, you can dispense with the bow, Gration. You're likely to keel over. Please, just sit down."

"Much obliged, my lord," the other mumbled in a gravely voice. Carefully he lowered his frame into a chair adjacent to the king and landed with a thud.

"If you grow any fatter, you're going to drop dead on me before you ever get a chance to tutor Theseus."

Gration eyed the child, reached over and mussed his hair. "He's growing like a weed. How old is the little heir apparent now?"

"Twenty-two months."

"You count the months?"

"I count the days. I waited a long time for him. It's a wonder you never had any of your own, Gration. You love to teach."

"Always afraid I wouldn't be able to feed them properly, my lord."

The twittering of a warbler floated in on the summer breeze. Aegeus hefted his son a little higher on his lap. Then he eyed Gration significantly. "You've heard?"

"I've heard."

"She's asked for sanctuary."

"Are you going to grant it?"

"I don't know. My council's against it. What do you think?"

"You and I usually disagree on things, my lord."

"I know. That's why I sent for you."

Gration scratched under his arm. "Will they come after her?"

"I don't think so. Despite his private feelings, Creon is a practical man. Even if he finds out that she's here, he knows Athens is as well fortified as Corinth. There won't be war over this."

"Then you're free to do what you'd like."

"What I'd like is to wash my hands of the whole awful business, but I can't. It is our tradition, our sacred tradition, to grant sanctuary to whoever asks, no matter what they've done. Moreover, I'm in her debt—for this fellow," he said, smiling at his son. "She interpreted the oracle for me. I followed her instructions, and Theseus was born before the year was out."

"Perhaps it was just a coincidence."

"Perhaps." Aegeus sighed. "When I was young, I was probably like everyone else. I had a morbid fascination with the misery of others, but I've reached the age when I'd rather hear about gardening, or cooking, or any mundane thing." The child's eyes grew heavy and began to close. Aegeus gathered him to his chest, one big hand at his back, another behind his head. "I'm thinking of the citizens right now. Will they accept her?"

"People have a marvelous capacity to forget, my lord," Gration replied, "as long as they're not personally involved and the offense occurred a comfortable distance away. They'll whisper for a while, but if she causes no trouble here—and I doubt she will—our countrymen will be quite happy to consign her transgression to the remote past, and attribute it to temporary madness."

"Madness," Aegeus mused. He shook his head. "No, Gration. I've looked into her eyes. She has a keen, sensitive mind, a lucid intelligence. She took innocent life, and she knew what she was doing. How can I condone that?"

"You don't have to condone it. All you have to do is understand it."

"What is there to understand? A wrong was done to her, yes, but every schoolboy knows that two wrongs don't make a right."

"Neither do a wrong and a right," Gration shrugged, "but we don't tell schoolboys that."

"Say what you will, revenge isn't justice."

"No, revenge is its hoary grandsire, and if we disavowed that unsavory ancestor long ago in the interest of societal order, we did so at the expense of instinct. Vengeance, I'm afraid, is more native to the heart than submission to the slow, haphazard machinery of law."

"But she hasn't just made Jason suffer. I know her, Gration. She'll suffer—until the day she dies—for what she's done."

"Ah, but you see, my lord, that's part of the contract. Revenge invites us to the evil banquet and bids us eat. Insufficient merely to damn the person who has wronged us, we have the unaccountable urge to damn ourselves into the bargain."

Aegeus contemplated his friend while he gently stroked his sleeping child. "She shows no remorse, none whatsoever."

"Don't look for any. If she claimed to be penitent, I would advise you to throw her from the wall."

"Instead, you're saying I should welcome her with open arms."

Gration's lips formed into a small, half-smile. "No, my lord. I'm saying you should grant her sanctuary."

* * *

Neither Jason nor Creon pursued Medea. King Creon died

in any case, some say of grief, soon after his daughter's death. With the loss of both members of the royal family, the Corinthian council overcame its objections, and so Jason finally became a king, though the death of his sons cast a shadow on his reign. In a tale too poetically apt to be true, he is said to have visited Iolcus late in his life to see the *Argo* one last time. The rotting hulk was drawn up on shore, and while Jason rested in the shade of its prow, recalling the adventure of his youth, the heavy carved figurehead of Hera crashed to earth and killed him. The Golden Fleece, object of Jason's long ago quest, vanished from history, but the portage road across the Isthmus of Corinth was used for centuries, far outlasting its builder, or even the memory that he was its builder.

Accounts of Medea's subsequent life vary. In one improbable tale she travels to Thebes and meets an ailing Hercules, who falls in love with her after she cures him with her drugs. In another tale it is King Aegeus who loves her, only later to banish her for fear she will poison his son, Theseus. In another she marries an unnamed, wealthy Eastern monarch who takes her back to her homeland in Colchis. And in still another it is Zeus himself who becomes ensnared, bestowing upon her eternal life in the Elysian Fields. Medea's actual fate was more prosaic. After being granted sanctuary, she lived out her life quietly and alone, a private citizen in Athens. But the fanciful stories agree with her true history in one significant respect: Medea was never punished for her crimes.

Confronted with this enigma, later ages made of Medea a myth. Her offense took on the protective garb of metaphor and became the archetypal expression of female rage. Thus humanity, in its incessant desire to know itself, stripped Medea's own humanity away. But crimes are not so easily dismissed in the living.

* * *

He made her cover her eyes. She felt his hand at her elbow guiding her up the rocky slope so she wouldn't stumble. When they reached the top of the hill, he said, "You can look now."

Slowly she lowered her hands. Small, gem-like, and gleaming brilliant white stood the temple—his temple, the temple he had

Richard Matturro

built—and as backdrop, a sweeping view of the mountains that rolled endlessly into the distant haze. He hurried her up the stairs. The hushed interior glowed with the muted light that bled through the columns. He continued to talk excitedly while she gazed at him. Finally he noticed that she wasn't listening any longer. "Well, what do you think, Mother?" he asked.

His angular face was framed with black curls. His deep, vibrant brown eyes and infectious smile nearly made her weep. She reached out to touch him. "I'm so proud of you ... Mermerus."

And he vanished.

Medea awoke, alone in her bed. Staring up into the darkness, she heard an owl hoot softly outside her window. There were no tears. Tears had long since forsaken her. There was only this hour, which she knew well. It was the phantom interval, the last watch before dawn when memories are unearthed, turned over, recast, as if some other conclusion were possible.

Daylight crept reluctantly into the room. She found herself padding to the shed. Her basket of tools was exactly where she had left it on the worktable. Nothing ever strayed now from where she put it. In the garden, dew glistened on the grape leaves, tiny droplets sliding down to the tapered points, but never quite falling off. As the sun rose higher in the sky, they resolved into air and disappeared.

The tall pyramidal stalk was covered with dozens of small, white flowers, more than yesterday. Unopened buds formed a pale green cone at the top that reached nearly to her knee. She ran her fingers over the tiny hairs that lined the tip, then crouched to inspect the bulb, which lay partly exposed on the earth. It needed water. Everything in the garden needed water at this season. Spring and fall brought the most flowers, but a few varieties, like this one, braved the drought to bloom in high summer.

"What have you got there?" a familiar voice asked.

"Sea squill, my lord," she responded before even turning around. She straightened up as Aegeus shuffled toward her, one hand on his cane, the other behind his back. His expression was kindly and grave at the same time, an attitude Medea knew he reserved only for her.

"Sea squill," he repeated. "Odd name. Pretty flower, though. Useful for anything?"

"It's good for the heart."

"Well, the heart needs all the help it can get. May we sit?"

She led him to a wooden bench in the shade of a cypress.

"Your garden is always lovely," he said, settling down. "I remember what this barren patch looked like when you moved in. How long ago now? Fifteen years? Sixteen?"

"Eighteen."

"Eighteen? Has it been that long? I still wish you'd decided to stay at the palace and take care of my garden instead."

"No you don't."

Aegeus smiled, didn't deny it. "Theseus was a toddler back then. Remember? Now he's a young hellion on his way to Crete. And I—." He took a breath. "I'm getting to be a very old man. But you seem to stay the same."

"Staying the same slows down time."

"Doubtful advantage in that, I dare say." He paused, became more serious. "The priestess tells me you would like to be made a votaress of Athena."

"If you have no objection, my lord."

"She also says your medicines effect more cures than the physicians."

"That's an exaggeration."

"Most sincere praise is." He leaned upon his cane and folded his hands over the knob, slowly opening and closing his fingers. "If you feel you owe Athens a debt, Medea, I should tell you that you've long since paid it. You've been a benefit to the city and its people. With all due respect to our patron goddess, Athena has enough votaries. There's no need for you to hole up in the temple. Your services are much more useful right here."

Medea rose. From the edge of the path she plucked a fern and held it very close to her face. "My sight is failing."

Aegeus looked at her. "I'm sorry, Medea. I didn't know."

"It doesn't really matter. I've seen enough. But I won't be able

Richard Matturro

to tend the garden much longer."

Putting his weight upon the cane Aegeus pulled himself to his feet. "If you want to become a votaress, I have no objection." He turned to leave, then stopped. "I think I complained to you once about how limited a king's power is. I can't forbid the rain to fall, or my son to fall ill. Worst of all, I can't forbid ghosts to haunt— nor should I try, I suppose." He sought her face. "You haven't found any peace, have you?"

Her crossed eyes bent inward. "I haven't looked for any."

With slow, halting gait he retreated down the path.

Medea called after him, "What is Theseus doing in Crete?"

"He's gone to take part in some infernal bull-leaping competition," Aegeus said over his shoulder. "He's at that age, you know."

Alone again, Medea sat under the cypress. She watched as a thrush hopped at the base of the tree probing with its beak among the crinkly dead leaves. Yes, she thought, at that age young men want to try everything. Bull-leaping. She had no idea what it was, but she was quite certain it would have appealed to Tisander.

She closed her eyes.

Richard Matturro, a native of Rye, New York, holds a doctorate in English with a specialization in Shakespeare and Greek Mythology. After sixteen years at the Albany *Times Union*, he now teaches literature at UAlbany and lives on an old farm in the foothills of the Berkshires. *Medea* is his sixth novel.
www.richardmatturro.com

Mary Trevor Thomas, a South Dakota native, is a graduate of Smith College and the School of the Museum of Fine Arts in Boston. Her work has been shown in Boston and Munich. She is currently a librarian in the Albany area.
www.marytrev.com